BLACK MAGIC

SHADOW OF THE PACK | BOOK 1

NICOLE AUSTEN

This book is a work of fiction. Names, characters, places, and incidents are either products of the author's imagination or are used fictitiously. Any resemblance to actual persons, living or dead, business establishments, events, or locales is entirely coincidental. The author makes no claims to, but instead acknowledges the trademarked status and trademark owners of the word marks mentioned in this work of fiction.

Copyright © 2022 by Nicole Austen

BLACK MAGIC by Nicole Austen
All rights reserved. Published in the United States of America by Month9Books, LLC.
No part of this book may be used or reproduced in any manner whatsoever without written permission of the publisher, except in the case of brief quotations embodied in critical articles and reviews.

Trade Paperback ISBN: 978-1-951710-69-9
ePub ISBN: 978-1-951710-70-5

Published by Month9Books, Raleigh, NC 27609
Illustrations by Sarah Sladk
Cover by Danielle Doolittle, DoElle Designs

Month9Books

Praise for *Black Magic: Shadow of the Pack*

"*Shadow of the Pack* is a thrilling tale about survival in the wild. Set in a world that is at once enchanting and dangerous, the story weaves a gripping drama of power, betrayal, and family. The Willow River wolves are real flesh-and-blood characters we care about, and the stakes in their fight for dominance are life and death. Austen's natural instinct for plot and action make her a wonderful new talent to watch."

—NYT Bestseller Soman Chainani, author of The School for Good and Evil series

"*Shadow of the Pack* is a joy to read, especially for those fascinated by wolves. Reading it brought me the same happy feeling I had when I first encountered *Watership Down*."

—NYT Bestseller Thomas Lennon, author of *Ronan Boyle and the Bridge of Riddles*

*Dad, who made everything possible,
this one's for you.*

BLACK MAGIC

SHADOW OF THE PACK | BOOK 1

Prologue

Moonlight touched the clearing where the pack prowled. It shone like silver dust on the forest leaves and rendered the grass beneath the wolves' paws in gray-green brilliance. It shimmered on their mottled backs and rounded ears, leaving their eyes to shine eerily from the shadows beneath their brows.

In the center of the clearing stood a black wolf with a patch of white on his chest. He was alone and exposed under the light of the moon. His large, golden eyes followed the movements of the other wolves. They circled him, stalking near the trees on either side of the clearing, passing in and out of shadow and light.

The black wolf's teeth were bared, shining bright white in the moonlight, and his tail was high and quivering with aggression. He was ready to fight for his life.

Hawk had known this would happen. It hadn't been long since he had left his birth pack and set off as a lone wolf. His search for food had led him deep into the heart of enemy territory. Willow River territory. Now, Hawk was surrounded by enemies, followers of the Old Way. Now, violence was his only option.

They had caught the scent of Hawk's old pack on his fur. They knew he had once considered the territory around Mud Lake his home, born into a pack that obeyed the New Way rather than adhering to the collective ancestral will. He would have to fight harder than most to prove himself worthy of joining them.

A low growl reverberated across the clearing. Hawk swept his eyes over the pack, searching for its source, and saw a large, green-eyed male standing near the forest's edge, teeth bared in a snarl. It was Alric, the alpha male of the Willow River pack.

The other wolves froze, heads tilted as they watched their leader. Alric took one step forward, then another, slowly approaching the lone wolf. Hawk stood motionless, his eyes narrowed. The slightest movement could provoke a fight.

There was triumph in Alric's eyes. Like he had already won. Hawk would make him pay for his overconfidence. No wolf, not even a powerful alpha such as Alric, could overcome Hawk's gift, a blessing he had carried with him since birth. But this gift from the ancestors was also his greatest secret. Revealing it to an Old Way alpha like Alric would be a mistake, especially if he wanted to make these wolves his packmates.

The rest of the pack began to inch forward, careful to stay far from Hawk's claws. Three wolves, all female. The Willow River pack was small and weak. They needed new members, especially strong males like Hawk. But the Old Way was harsh, and it never compromised, not even when the survival of the pack depended on it. Hawk would have to fight to prove his worth.

For a moment, everything was quiet and still. The only sounds were the distant chirping of crickets, the whisper of a breeze, and the wolves' soft panting as they faced off in the center of the clearing. Their breaths rose in faint white mist from their mouths, swirling together in the brisk night air.

A violent growl broke the silence as the largest of the females stepped forward, eyes narrowed in a challenge. Hawk could sense her anticipation, her eagerness to prove her strength to her alpha. She was only a subordinate, a mid-ranking wolf, but her ambition was clear. The lone wolf stretched back the corners of his mouth and bared his teeth in a wolf grin, mocking her. She'd soon regret facing him.

The female was unfazed. She sprang forward and knocked Hawk to the ground. She was stronger than he had expected, pinning him beneath her claws, smothering his face in her thick white fur. He thrashed beneath her, unable to breathe. Panic rushed through him, and he felt something deep inside his body begin to rise to the surface.

A single golden spark danced across his vision, and he lashed out with incredible strength, a single kick of his hind legs throwing the white-furred female halfway across the clearing.

Hawk closed his eyes and pushed down the wild surge of magic. The other wolves stared at the white female as she shakily got to her paws. Blinded by fear for their packmate, the wolves were oblivious to Hawk's attempts to tame the energy inside him.

With another furious growl, the female charged. Her claws flashed through the air, glimmering in the moonlight, as Hawk whirled out of the way. She stumbled forward, off-balance. Hawk lunged.

Moments later, all that could be seen was a writhing ball of fur rolling back and forth across the ground. The two wolves clawed and bit at each other, struggling to pin their opponent and gain the advantage. Alric moved forward to protect his packmate, then shrank back again as Hawk's claws raked through the fur on his chest and barely missed his skin. The fight was too heated for him to intervene. Or perhaps he just wanted to see who would prevail.

Though Hawk was taking care to control his magic this time, he was still the more experienced fighter, and his size gave him an edge. The white female kicked and struggled, but Hawk was too strong. Soon, he had his teeth around her throat. He began to bite down, fangs cutting through her fur and digging into her skin.

Then he remembered what he was fighting for. Alric would never accept him into the pack if he killed one of its members.

Hawk released his grip on the female and backed away. Silently, he turned to look at Alric. The hairs on his back stood on end, and his exposed teeth flashed like blades.

The female got up. Her white coat was matted with blood and dust. A few shallow scratches ran along her side, and the fur around the bite-marks on her neck was stained red. She lowered her head and whined at Hawk, acknowledging his victory and expressing her gratitude at his mercy.

With a short, low howl and a wave of his tail, Alric

invited Hawk into the Willow River pack. He would be its beta, higher in status than all but the alpha male and female.

Hawk raised his head in triumph. He had doubted the Old Way at first, but perhaps it was the ancestors' desire that he join such a group of wolves. Finally, he would live in a pack where his strength was appreciated. Where the will of the ancestors was held above all other things. Where the weak, the dangerous, and the sacrilegious were cast out or killed without hesitation, and the pack was guided by the values of countless generations that had come before them.

For a moment, Hawk felt a flicker of regret. He was leaving behind so much. His home, his way of life, his family. His poor, timid sister Lily, trapped in their birth pack with such a tyrannical leader ...

Hawk pushed his guilt away. He would be happy in this new pack, living a life in service of the ancestors. And perhaps, once he had won Alric's trust, Lily could join him.

Or maybe Hawk's new packmates would discover his secret abilities, and he would meet an entirely different end.

Chapter 1

It was dark in the valley by the stream.

Rain fell in a never-ending sheet of frigid droplets. Lightning flashed, occasionally striking one of the trees in the forest and setting it ablaze, a rapid claw slash of fire which was quickly extinguished by the rain. The heavy wind roared, an invisible force sweeping through the trees, uprooting the ones with the weakest roots.

Inside a hole dug into a small hill near the stream was a shivering wolf. She crouched at the back of her den, head lying flat on the damp soil, fur draped in shadows. Lightning streaked her pale gray pelt with brightness, momentarily illuminating yellow eyes wide with terror. Her name was Lora.

She wasn't shivering from the cold. Wolves had thick coats, and hers was especially dense, as her ancestors were from the far north. In winter, she was as bushy as a bear, and her tail streamed out behind her like a wild horse's when she ran.

Lora shivered because she was giving birth.

All she could hear was howling wind, battering rain,

and cracking thunder. And for a moment, she felt alone. She knew her pack was just outside the den, waiting and worrying, but in her pain, she couldn't sense them. She felt only the warm, sweet brightness of oblivion tearing harder and harder at her mind.

As her vision flickered and dimmed, the thought of her mate and daughter pulled her away from the light and back into the darkness of the world.

Outside the den, three wolves paced, paws slapping against the thin fingers of water that rolled down the hill to the stream. Their ears were pricked, though they could hear nothing but the storm, and their eyes glowed in the darkness as they watched the small entrance to the hole in the ground where Lora was birthing her pups. A fourth wolf stood in front of them, larger than his packmates, quiet and still.

This wolf was a magnificent creature, though his fur hung limp and wet from the rain. He was dusty brown with streaks of copper and gray, like a sheer cliff face. His back was heavily flecked with color, his belly almost white. He seemed to slump just a bit, as though the burden of leading his pack for three long years was weighing him down. His eyes were the color of springtime leaves, and now they were narrowed to slits as he stared unblinkingly at the den.

This was Alric, Lora's mate, the alpha male and leader of the Willow River pack.

Another thin web of lightning partitioned the sky, striking a tree in the forest. Alric turned his head and watched as the fire blazed for a moment, glowing like a torch in the rain, before the water snuffed it out in a haze of smoke.

The storm was wreaking havoc on the entire valley. The forest on either side of the den site was constantly assailed by lightning, its trees blown over by the wind. On the other side of the stream, the meadow where the herds often grazed had been reduced to a muddy wasteland, pockmarked with holes where the elks' sharp hooves had penetrated the ground's sticky surface.

The den itself had been dug into the side of a hill facing the stream, with a long stretch of open area between it and the willow trees that lined the water's edge. The fronds of the willows were tossed about in the ever-changing wind, desperately clinging to their trees as the storm whipped them through the air like thin, leafy banners. Their trunks were submerged in a foot of water, bending but never breaking.

In the five years Alric had lived, he had never seen a storm like this. It had to be the work of the ancestors. They sent storms and famines to show their displeasure and brought clear days and elk herds when they were happy. If they were angry at Alric and his pack, what did that mean for Lora and her pups? Would the ancestors steal their lives, rip them away from their packmates like willow fronds ripped from their trees?

Alric pricked his ears, listening for a sign. But he could hear nothing over the wind and rain. He could smell nothing above the scents of fire and water and his packmates' fear. And he felt alone.

Alric had been leading the Willow River pack for nearly three years. All the wolves obeyed him, even his mate Lora, though she was older than him and probably wiser. But it was the alpha male, not his mate, who led the pack. And his strongest son would follow him. That was the way it had been for generations, the Old Way.

On the surface, the Old Way was a collection of laws, ceremonies, and customs that governed the lives of the wolves that followed it. But it was also a system of belief, an entire way of thinking, all guided by a strict adherence to the will of the ancestors.

Alric's father had taught him to respect the ancestors, to heed their signs and follow their laws. Some neighboring packs did things differently, but they had always been Alric's enemies. The North River and Mud Lake packs had been rivals of Willow River for generations. They had cast aside the ancient customs of the wolf and betrayed the ancestors, proving their depravity time and time again. The new leader of the Mud Lake pack had gone so far as to exile her own father.

The thunder crashed again, like the horns of rutting bull elk cracking together in a rhythmic dance for dominance.

Alric shivered, then reminded himself that he had to remain perfectly still. A leader who wanted to keep control of his pack could not appear weak.

One wolf was watching Alric with hard golden eyes, as though already plotting his downfall. Alric sensed the hostile gaze and whipped his head around, glaring at a black male with a white patch on his chest. Hawk. The alpha rumbled out a low growl. It had been three seasons since Hawk joined the pack, a summer, fall, and winter of growing animosity. Hawk was already the pack's beta, Alric's second in command, but he wasn't content with his position. He wanted more.

Alric's bright green eyes stood out like shining emeralds in the darkness. Hawk looked away. He wasn't ready to challenge the alpha male. They waited on the birth of his litter now, but should Alric die before producing an heir, Hawk would become the new leader. And the storm was not an auspicious sign for the alpha's pups.

Alric watched as Hawk's eyes narrowed to slits. He knew his beta wasn't loyal to him, but Hawk was the only other male in the pack. The benefits of having a strong second-in-command outweighed the risks. For now.

A piercing yip sounded from within the den, louder than the wind and rain, cutting through Alric's mind like a tooth. His ear twitched.

Beside Alric, a small gray and silver female whined, her

thick fur clinging to her ribs like sap to tree bark and her ears pinned back. Her eyes were the same color as Alric's, bright green, but they were glazed over with fear.

Irritated, Alric turned to the female and shoved his ears forward, baring his teeth. That was all it took for her to quiet down.

This wolf was Rynna, Alric's daughter and the sole survivor of Lora's first litter. She had her mother's unusual fur, not a hint of brown or red in it, only a bluish, misty sheen. She stared down at her paws, wondering if Lora would live.

After what had happened the past two springs, no wolf was sure.

Memories bombarded Rynna: wet splinters digging into her paws, a cold current dragging at her fur, fear and pain, and the sound of her siblings' whimpers from somewhere behind her, out of reach.

All three of her brothers had died. And the year after that, Lora had given birth to just a single stillborn pup. Rynna could still hear her father's sorrowful howling.

Rynna wondered what Alric would do if Lora failed again. An alpha female was only just past her prime at six years of age, but Lora was now a weaker wolf than most. Like many alpha females, she led the hunt, and she had been kicked countless times by elk. She had also barely survived two births, and an illness had almost claimed her life the previous winter. She walked with a wavering in her step, like a strong gust of wind could blow her away.

Alric glanced first at Rynna, then at the den. He knew why Rynna was worried. He would have to find a new alpha female if Lora was unable to give him the male heir he so desperately needed. The favor of the ancestors was crucial to their survival. If he were forced to abandon the Old Way, the long-dead wolves in the sky would not be pleased.

Their fate was already in doubt. There were four wolves waiting in the dark outside the den, and they were each as silent as a shadow. They and Lora were all that remained of the Willow River pack, with only one pup surviving to adulthood over the past two years. Alric was thankful for Hawk and Wyanet, the dispersal wolves who had joined his pack. Without them, he and Lora and his timid daughter would have to hold down a territory far too big for them to defend.

Finally, the wind began to fade, and the thunder sank into the distance. The willow fronds, no longer in the storm's grasp, swayed gently on their branches as though nothing had happened. One, torn from its branch by the wind, landed as soft as a feather at Alric's paws. The only sound now was the gentle patter of rain. No noise came from the den. Alric couldn't move. He couldn't breathe. His fear kept him frozen.

And then a dappled gray and silver head emerged from the hole in the ground. Lora's pale eyes were dull with exhaustion, but there was a hint of triumph there as well. Her ears were pricked up and her tail held aloft and wagging, signaling that all was well.

The pack suddenly came alive. All of them, even Alric, began shivering with excitement, wagging their tails and spinning in circles like they were pups themselves. Joyful whimpers filled the clearing, and playful paws slapped against the muddy ground as the wolves danced. Their belly fur still dripped, and raindrops still drummed thick and fast on their skulls, but they hardly noticed. Rynna and Wyanet, the pack's young subordinate females, began a game of wolf tag, which was enthusiastically joined by the two males.

None of them went near the den. None of them dared. Lora would drive away any wolf who got too close to the den before the pups were ready to emerge. This was an Old Way tradition which Alric had no choice but to respect. It would be three weeks before he would meet his offspring.

Lora would leave her pups only to feed off previous kills, or pack members would drop choice bits of meat at the den mouth for her. In her absence, Alric would lead the hunts.

For Willow River's alpha male, it would be a long three weeks.

Chapter 2

It was warm in the den under the ground. The rain had finally stopped, and everything smelled new and clean. Safe.

Lora knew that if anything should threaten her or her pups, Alric would leap upon it as quick as a rabbit and tear it limb from limb with the ferocity of a cougar. No harm could befall them, not with him standing guard.

Inside the den, the air was damp, like early morning. The earthworms were pushing their way out of the dirt to absorb the last drops of rain that had reached the den floor. Lora could feel them wriggling beneath her, but all her attention was focused on the pups, and she paid them no mind.

There were four newborn pups. Lora could smell each one of them clearly and feel their paws churning against her belly. It was dark in the den, but she was a wolf, and she could easily make out their small, rounded bodies. Their eyes were shut and would not open for two weeks. Every few moments, one of them whined or whimpered or yelped. A good sign. All four pups were strong. The ancestors must be watching over her.

But she still felt a tiny prickle of foreboding. Her fur stood on end, and she pressed her ears to the back of her head fearfully. It was still nighttime, and the moonlight couldn't quite reach the bottom of the den. She had no way to know what her pups looked like until morning.

As they grew and acquired specific diets and behaviors, each pup would develop their own distinct smell, easily identified by the keen noses of their packmates. For now, Lora could only determine their genders—two males and two females. Alric had been waiting so long for an heir, and it seemed that she had finally given him one. It had been a long time since Lora had seen his red-tinged muzzle open wide in a wolf grin, or his tail swish back and forth in joy. She wanted these pups to make him happy for once. But she couldn't be sure they would until she saw them in the light of day.

The Old Way was built on superstition, a thousand seasons worth of knowledge and belief. Red wolves were thought to have fiery tempers, silver wolves were wise, wolves with darker coats were sly and shifty, and white wolves were pure of heart. And there were other, darker superstitions, which resided deep at the core of the pack's memory.

The Willow River pack considered such knowledge to be simple instinct. Individual wolves would make observations and file them away in their memory. Other wolves would pick up on this through intuition and remember it as well. When one wolf focused hard enough on a memory or a feeling, it trickled into the minds of those nearby. Information was even passed between packs in this way.

It was common knowledge among all packs that pups were born dark brown and developed more colorful and diverse coats as they grew. Yet lately, there had been troubling news from the Willow River pack's neighbors of pups with fur like solid shadows. An omen of dark magic.

Lora let out a puff of breath through her nose and repressed a shiver. She had survived the birth and given Alric two sons for heirs, but she was still afraid for her pups. Hopefully, seeing them in daylight would put all of her fears to rest.

A few scarce rays of sunlight were starting to reach the den, darting inside as quick as deer hooves. Color began to saturate Lora's vision, revealing hints at how its pattern might drape the fur of her pups.

The largest of them was a male, with the typical dark brown coat of a young pup. Like the rest of his siblings, his fur was soft, spiky, and slightly damp, and his ears rounded over the top of his head. He seemed as fierce as a bear cub. He drank milk like it was his last meal, and every so often he would turn to kick at one of his siblings, trying to keep the food for himself. The perfect heir. Alric would be pleased indeed.

Next to the little bear-pup was another male, paler in color than the first. As Lora watched, his larger brother shoved him aside with a clumsy kick, throwing loose soil into the air. The lighter-furred male whimpered, his high-pitched squeak echoing around the den like birdsong. When he tried to roll away from the reach of his brother, he was butted aside by one of his sisters. As he crawled, whining, back towards his mother, Lora noticed something gleaming on his forehead. An almost-white mark glowed softly in the semi-darkness of the den, its gentle, pulsing light drowning Lora in a rush of calm. She stared with wide yellow eyes for a moment, before reluctantly averting her gaze, fur prickling as she contemplated the meaning of the strange pale marking.

The third pup, a female, was nestled close to her much larger brothers. She was the smallest pup, but she had one of the best feeding spots, which she was holding onto through sheer determination. Her eyes were shut tight, her little muzzle wrinkled in concentration as her paws dug into the soil. She was unmovable. Every time the largest male would try to shove her out of the way, she would shove back, never giving any ground.

Three beautiful, perfect pups.

While Lora admired her offspring, sunlight crept deeper into the den, finally settling on the final pup curled farthest from the entrance. When Lora's eyes flicked to the fourth pup, fear flooded through her so strongly that she had to look away.

The female huddled by the back wall of the den, nosing around vainly in search of her mother's milk, blocked by her wriggling siblings. Her whines were more distressed than the others', like she was crying for help. Her fur stuck to her sleek frame. Her muzzle was sharp and angled, her face thin. There was no puppy fat, only sharp, jutting bone. The pup's fur was pure black.

Darkness crept up around the edges of Lora's vision, and all of her senses began to fade away. She could barely smell the warm scent of her own milk, barely hear the whining of her newly born pups, barely feel their soft fur brushing against her own. She was being dragged towards unconsciousness, drowning, fading … Desperately, she fought, lying still on the den floor until her light-headedness slipped away like the storm had only hours before.

Once the feeling of shock receded, terror set in. Lora's breaths surged like tidal waves in her chest, her paws scrabbling against the den's floor. The walls suddenly felt too close, the air too thin. She lunged towards the den entrance, overcome by the need to run far away from her pure black daughter. To forget this birth had ever happened, because the triumph of bearing two sons didn't matter now. The happiness she had felt just moments ago was dust, completely eclipsed by her devastation at the sight of his fourth pup. Every instinct urged her to get away.

But Lora fought her instincts. Her pups still needed her. She quieted them with a comforting whimper, keeping her head down so as not to bump it on the low ceiling of the den, and tentatively approached the pure black female. The strange pup shrank back like a turtle retreating into its shell. Lora nosed the pup again and again and stared at her, hoping she would come to a different conclusion. But no, it wasn't a trick of the light. This was a pure black pup, not a paler mark on her.

Lora returned to her place by the other pups, panting desperately as she searched for an explanation. But in the countless seasons since wolves came into being, there had only ever been one explanation for a pure black pup.

She knew what tradition demanded of her. She should take her daughter and drown her in the stream. All she would have to do was stand over the rushing water and let go. The pack would celebrate the birth of Alric's heirs, ignorant of what Lora had created and what she had done.

The black pup had wiggled her way up to join her siblings and was peacefully drinking milk. Both her eyes were closed now, and her tiny paws clumsily kneaded her mother's belly. Save her ink-black fur and angular features, she seemed like any other pup.

Most wolves in the pack believed in the lessons taught by their ancestors, the wolves who now dwelled in the skies. But at the back of her mind, Lora had always doubted their existence.

She could never kill her own pup. She wouldn't.

She knew her innocent daughter couldn't be the dark creature the ancestors so feared.

But that didn't make her any less afraid. Over and over again, Lora imagined the look on her beloved Alric's face when he saw what she had brought into the world.

Chapter 3

Three weeks dragged by, and the morning when Alric would meet his pups finally arrived.

The thaw that had begun a few weeks before the pups were born was finally over. Rather than muddy snow lying on the ground in patches, a blanket of trilliums rose from the forest floor. The meadow was again full of green, and the monarch butterflies had returned from the south to complete their yearly migration.

The elk herd had been lured back to Willow River territory by all this tempting vegetation, so Alric knew the pack would have plenty to eat.

It was midmorning, and Alric sat outside the den, staring wide-eyed at its opening. Flashes of light winked at the corners of his eyes, where the dew lay sparkling on the forest grass. The woods were bright and innocent, and were it any other day, Alric would spend hours walking among the trees. But he wouldn't miss the chance to finally meet his pups for anything.

Hours passed. The last of the rainwater from the storm

had finally been reclaimed by the clouds, so the ground Alric's claws dug into was hard-packed and dryer than bone. The sun hammered down on his back, sucking up the dew and making his pelt itch.

He had been waiting all day. Surely his packmates were beginning to worry about him. But Alric was determined to sit here all afternoon and all night if necessary.

Lifting his head and wagging his tail in excitement, Alric spotted a hint of gray by the den entrance. He leaned forward, barely able to contain his anticipation.

Lora poked her muzzle out of the den, wrinkling her nose and squinting in the light. She trotted out, paws throwing up a cloud of dust in Alric's face as she passed him by. Ignoring her mate, she bent her head to lap up some water from the stream. She clearly had no plans to reveal her pups anytime soon.

She made it halfway back to the den before Alric's loud whine stopped her. They stared at each other. Alric's expression was open and pleading, but Lora held her head high and dismissed him with a flick of her tail. Her gaze was a sharp and discerning, like a fox who'd sensed a mouse beneath the snow. Alric drew himself up and stepped forward, incredulous. His mate had never disobeyed a command of his before. Why was she so desperate to keep her pups in the den? Had she failed to produce a male heir yet again?

He had waited for three whole weeks, and he would wait

no longer. His mouth curled, exposing a long, shining tooth.

Lora didn't move. She was trembling slightly, weakened by her old injuries and the sicknesses and births she had survived. Yet her ears were pointed straight up, her head and tail held high. An expression of dominance. Alric opened his mouth to reveal the rest of his teeth. He was the leader of this pack. If his mate continued to resist him, she would be disobeying the Old Way and defying the ancestors themselves.

With that, Lora relented. She yipped, the shrill sound full of apprehension.

All the tension drained out of Alric. His tail wagged so fast it was a blur. Lora rubbed her cheek against his, then turned to get the pups. He evened out his stance, raised his head, and howled. His voice started off high and joyful, then slowly faded down into a strong, deep note, a note of anticipation. The rest of the pack tilted their heads at him, listening in silent reverence.

Rynna trotted over from where she had been dozing on the other side of the den site and stood beside him, a wolf grin spreading across her face. Alric's note slowly faded to silence, like a trickle of water drying out. When he raised his head to howl again, Rynna joined the song, her voice as high and wavering as the white butterfly that flitted above the den in lazy circles. Their howls seemed to spiral up to the clouds, soaring higher and higher, then slowly falling like snow to the ground.

While Lora slipped back into the den, Wyanet and Hawk bounded over and joined in. Soon the air buzzed with the voices of wolves. Their paws danced as they moved around each other joyfully, and their fur flowed around their necks in the heavy breeze. Their howls climbed slowly up and down the scale, slipping effortlessly between gorgeous harmonies and eerie, dissonant chords. Often, a wolf would open their eyes and stop howling for a moment, twisting in a small circle and yipping madly in excitement.

The wolves' happiness stemmed only partially from the pups. Much of it came from the howl itself. The magnificent sense of unity that came from joining together in song was enough to fill any wolf with joy.

The pack's rally faltered as Lora reemerged, the fur on her back brushing against the upper lip of the den. She seemed hesitant, and the pack could smell her fear. Alric stifled a whimper. Something was wrong.

Lora turned and uttered a soft cry of encouragement. Several little squeaks answered.

The first pup to emerge from the den looked exceedingly small to Alric. He narrowed his eyes, wondering if this was why Lora was so nervous. A small female leading the way suggested an entire litter of females, possibly even tinier than this one. But she was healthy and strong. She held her head and tail high, ignoring the heat and the dust and the insects that fluttered distractingly around her nose. Though she tripped and teetered on clumsy puppy paws, there was an impression of royalty in her proud gaze. She made straight for Alric, and when he lowered his head, she licked his mouth in wolf tribute. The whole pack shivered with happiness.

The little pup looked like all others did at that age. She had a short snout and ears stuck to the sides of her head, with four stubby legs that she waddled around on. The hue of her dark brown pup coat would thicken and change color as she grew, marking her slow transition to adulthood. Her eyes were large and innocent, blue like the eyes of all young pups.

Alric glanced at Lora, then back at the tiny female, who was still staring up at him with her big, sky-blue eyes. He had been hoping for a male, but he couldn't help feeling a wave of affection for his bold little daughter.

The sounds of a scuffle broke out from inside the den. A playful growl, a whine, the sound of claws scraping against stone … the pack leaned forward eagerly as a large male pup barreled into the clearing. He shot past Alric and nearly careened into the trunk of a willow tree. He skidded to a halt just in time, panting and wagging his tail. He had fought his way past his siblings in his eagerness to leave the confines of the den.

Alric tilted his head at the male. He, too, had the dark brown fur of a young pup. His eyes were also blue, though not the same blindingly pale shade as his sister's. Alric's early apprehension faded away, a single flake of snow under a blazing summer sun. The next pup was seconds behind the big male, but Alric barely spared him a glance. He was too fixated on his larger son. Finally, he had an heir worthy of leading the pack after him.

Alric grinned at the big male, his hopes attaching themselves to the pup like the tendrils of a vine clinging to stone.

But as the fourth pup emerged, Alric's attention was wrenched away from his new favorite.

The pack froze. Their happy whimpers turned abruptly to silence. Their wagging tails dropped and hung still.

The fourth pup, a medium-sized female, had fur the color of onyx. Its thick folds were draped in shadows. Her eyes were not blue. They were dark orange, the color of rust, and their stare seemed to stab through Alric's skin and muscle and see into him, through him.

Pure black wolves were the servants and spies of ancestors with blackened hearts who ruled the furthest reaches of the skies. They were rumored to have dark powers beyond imagining. Wolves were often granted more benign magic by ancestors who had lived lives of honor, duty, and loyalty, the long-dead souls who were worshipped and obeyed by the followers of the Old Way. But there were other ancestors, the spirits of the cruel and traitorous, who every so often selected a wolf in the living world to do their bidding. A wolf with power over death itself.

While the pack remained frozen with fear, Lora surreptitiously scanned for any streak of brown that might catch the sun's rays and spare her pup. Still seeing no strands of hope, she grinned at the pack as though nothing was wrong. Their shock cracked like melting ice. They loped forward and began to inspect the three normal pups, licking them, playing with them, and yipping joyfully like they were pups themselves.

None of them would go near the black pup.

Even Hawk, his own fur so dark brown it was almost black, stayed away. The patch of white on his chest had saved him from being labeled a bearer of dark magic. He felt no sympathy for the pup. In fact, he was afraid of her. There was something very wrong about her, something the whole pack felt.

Hawk shuddered. He had spent his whole life obeying the code of the ancestors. They had rules for situations like these. The black pup should be dead, drowned in the stream. Surely, Alric would do what his mate could not. The alpha male wasn't quite as devoted to the ancestors as Hawk was, but he followed their laws. He would not betray them.

Hawk watched the alpha male out of the corner of his eye. Alric was playing with his favorite son, running circles around the boisterous pup. Hawk would do anything for the ancestors, yet his position as Alric's heir was still being usurped by nothing but a newborn.

Lora, meanwhile, saw how the pack looked at her. Like she had done something terrible, something that had put them all in danger. She sat watching the other wolves play, a low growl rumbling at the base of her throat. She refused to feel guilty for keeping her daughter alive. The black-furred female hadn't done anything wrong.

After a few minutes of playing with his heir, Alric approached Lora on heavy paws. His eyes were narrowed, but regret hid beneath the anger in his stare. He didn't want to do this. He had no choice.

It was Lora's fault. She had put him in this position, and it made him want to rip every willow frond at the den site to pieces.

Lora lowered her gaze in submission, fur standing on end. When she looked up again, she saw the rage in his eyes. Such hatred ... directed at her? Her daughter? She took a fearful step back, the ground beneath her paws suddenly cold.

Alric slowly turned towards the black pup. She was sitting in front of the den, silently watching her siblings play with those unsettling rust-colored eyes. Dust swirled up around her in strange shapes, phantom wolves materializing at her summons. Or perhaps that was only Alric's imagination.

He was the one wolf who could end this problem for his pack. Lora should have done it the day this dark pup was born, but she hadn't. And so it fell on Alric's shoulders to right the wrong, to appease the ancestors.

Alric was hesitant, but he had to put his trust in the ancestors' wisdom and carry out their will. He had a duty to protect his pack.

The pup raised her head and looked at him. She gazed into his eyes with a glassy stare that was wide and blank and empty. Like she was dreaming. What kind of monster had Alric fathered?

He took a step towards the pup.

With a ferocious snarl, Lora leapt between Alric and her daughter. Her tail was raised and shivering with aggression, her yellow eyes blazing. With her ears pinned to the sides of her head and her body lowered in a fighting stance, Lora made her choice.

The alpha male's ears pricked in surprise. And then he realized what he had been about to do. Was this really the will of the ancestors?

It had to be. Otherwise, everything he had been taught as a pup was wrong.

But he could not fight his own mate. He would find another way. He sat down and began grooming his fur as though nothing had happened.

Lora might be the pup's mother, but Alric was the leader of the pack. She shouldn't stop him from doing his duty. Yet part of him was happy that she had.

Chapter 4

Despite the air of fear and uncertainty surrounding the black pup, the pack lavished attention on the others.

Rynna had never met a pup besides her lost brothers, so for her, the newborns were a fresh delight. She had already found a playmate in the smaller of the two male pups, who tried over and over again to tackle Rynna, even though she was ten times his size. She eventually let him win, flopping onto the ground and throwing up a huge cloud of dust. Her younger brother's joyful whines of triumph more than made up for the face full of dirt.

Wyanet and Hawk played wolf tag with the tiny female, running slowly so she could keep up. This game only added to the cloud of dust that hung over the den site, and soon most of the pack had collapsed onto the ground, grinning and sneezing.

All but Alric and his heir, who kept playing, wrestling by the stream. Alric had almost forgotten the black-furred female. He felt like a pup again.

The pack played for hours before Alric reluctantly put an end to their celebration with a ringing howl that gathered the wolves around him. Their faces glowed, their pelts were coated in dust, and their tails were wagging.

Alric rose up into an alpha's pose, the spring sunlight bringing out the red in his fur. Wyanet and Rynna bounded forward, tails between their legs, hindquarters nearly brushing the ground, and covered his muzzle in licks of admiration. Hawk and Lora, who ranked higher than the subordinates, joined in after a moment, each giving Alric a single lick as tribute. Even the pups crowded in instinctively. Alric had cemented his position as alpha by fathering a healthy litter, and now his packmates were showing their respect.

Alric lowered his head so the pups could lick it, grinning. He could feel his position solidifying, the pack unifying around him, the shadow of the black pup fading into the background.

Alric turned and led his energetic pack up the grassy hill behind the den. The sky was cloudless and as blue as a jay's wing. The sun beat down heavily, trying to trample the wolves with its heat as an elk might do with its hooves.

Lora called the pups with a quiet yap, and they waddled up the hill on tiny paws. It was time for them to receive their names.

The large male pup beat his siblings up the hill with ease, and Alric wagged his tail. The rest of the pups were right behind him. The five adults clustered around them, making observations with sharp eyes. Lora kept the smallest female to herself, wanting to give her a name that fit her character. Hawk, Rynna, and Wyanet crowded around the second male pup. The black pup wandered towards the tree line, but no wolf called her back. That left Alric with his favorite new son.

Alric knew that his packmates were letting him name this pup on his own. They realized how important the heir was. It meant continuing his family's legacy, ensuring that it would carry on to the next generation. It meant staying true to the Old Way and to the ancestors.

In every way, this male was perfect. His dark brown fur was streaked with red, the same as Alric's, and he was nearly twice the size of his siblings. His blue-gray eyes had tiny flecks of green. He seemed excited, running back and forth across the grass, experiencing the world for the first time. As his father examined him, the pup skidded to a stop and stepped closer to Alric, batting at his front leg with oversized puppy paws.

Alric grinned and held the pup's new name at the forefront of his mind. He would be called Greatpaw.

Through the special intuition that bound all wolves together, Lora became aware of her son's name. She turned towards Alric, grinning. She was ready to forgive her mate for what he had tried to do. Surely, he would never attempt to harm the pup again, not after learning how Lora felt about it. But Alric only stared at her, his expression unreadable.

Lora bowed her head and turned away. If Alric didn't want her forgiveness, then so be it. There was nothing she could do now but wait and hope. Maybe he would eventually accept his daughter. But challenging him directly would only make things worse. He'd never accept advice from a wolf who made him look weak in front of his pack.

Lora couldn't dwell on it now. She turned away from her mate and looked into the pale blue eyes of her tiny daughter, the one who had clung so hard to life even though she was the smallest. This pup represented true strength and perseverance. Lora saw such determination within that pale blue that the pup became known as Ice Eyes.

Hawk, Rynna, and Wyanet struggled to decide on a name for the third pup. He was paler than his siblings, his fur a silky chestnut color. And there was that white mark on his forehead, which the wolves were fixated on. It made them feel calm and happy. They stared at it for several moments before Hawk ripped his eyes away and growled. He could see submission in the bearing of this pup. He had watched the pale-furred male's siblings push him around, saw him give up without a fight. This pup was weak. But perhaps, if Hawk gave him a fierce name, he would be inspired to grow stronger.

Rynna turned and growled at him, her eyes narrowed

to the thickness of a claw. Hawk's eyes widened in surprise. He was the beta, and Rynna had no right to show him such disrespect. But before he could act, Rynna named the pup with a strong mental declaration. He would be called Star.

Rynna had already grown attached to her younger brother. He seemed so sweet, so innocent, much like her favorite brother and best friend from when she was younger. That pup had died. A pup's life was a fragile thing. Star shouldn't waste the time he had been given. He should live his life as himself, not as what Hawk or even Alric wanted him to be.

The name was perfect. The bright sunlight reflected off the pale marking on Star's forehead, making it shine with all the brilliance of the night sky.

Hawk snarled. Star had been named. There was nothing he could do about it now.

The adults stepped away from the three pups and glanced at each other. There was still one more to name.

Alric turned towards the black pup. He knew what he had to do. This was something Lora couldn't deny him.

The black-furred female was sitting at the edge of the forest, looking into the distance with that same vacant stare. There was something happy in it, some hint of contentment, but the way her strange, wide eyes had glassed over sent a chill through Alric's skin. He gave her a name with one accusatory glance. She would be Mala, a title reserved for the corrupted servants of the darkest ancestors. It was a warning to all wolves who approached her that she had the potential for dark magic. This was Alric's way of declaring her a cursed one, an outcast in her own pack.

Mala was named. But even as Lora's eyes widened with shock and sadness, even as Alric turned away with a snarl on his face, the pup didn't blink.

Chapter 5

The sun had begun to dip beneath the horizon as Mala sat at the edge of the forest, a single cricket chirping next to her ear. Shadows spread slowly across the den site, patching the valley in stripes of gray and black. The pups had been named only a few hours previously, but to Mala it felt like an eternity. She had been sitting like this for a long time, absorbing the thoughts of the wolves around her.

Now that the pups had been named, they could perceive the pack's silent mental communication. Curious little Mala listened the closest.

When she had emerged from the den and seen the forest for the first time, she had desperately wanted to explore it, but she was too small, and Lora wouldn't let her out of sight. She could hear the wind rustling the tree branches behind her. She could smell the soft, calming scent of bark and dead leaves. She wished she were deep inside the forest, with the rustling and the lovely smells all around her, but instead she sat with the trees at her back.

Instead of watching the forest, she watched her siblings play.

They were too busy to notice her, engrossed in ambushing their mother. Lora lay in a patch of shade. Her flank rose and fell as she breathed, and her gray fur blended in with the trees behind her as their shadows lengthened. She seemed oblivious to the trio of pups silently planning their attack.

Ice Eyes directed the operation, using tail signals to tell her brothers where to go. With a sharp mental command and a flick of her tail, she ordered Star to distract Lora. Star wrinkled his nose, unhappy with the task he had been given but unwilling to argue with Ice Eyes. Instead, he whined softly at his mother, begging for her attention. Lora turned her head to look at him, leaving herself vulnerable to attack. Ice Eyes and Greatpaw slowly crept forward, placing their paws lightly and keeping their heads low. When they were close enough, Ice Eyes gave the signal to attack.

Mala watched, riveted, as the two pups leapt. Lora bolted upright, yipping in surprise, but Greatpaw's weight pinned her down again. She squirmed and flailed her paws, careful not to smack her pups too hard. Star jumped into the fray, and soon, the three pups and their mother were tussling on the ground in a big heap.

But Mala didn't want to play. She preferred observing. There was a nice breeze, the sun was setting, and the stars were just beginning to come out. It was pleasant enough to sit and watch her family without joining in.

A few moments later, the pups' energy was spent. They fell into a pile next to Lora, with Star on the bottom, Ice Eyes on the top, and Greatpaw happily sandwiched in between.

Suddenly, Mala felt lonely. Her father, Alric, was sitting on the hill above the den, gazing up at the rising crescent moon. Mala waddled towards him, whimpering a happy greeting and hoping his reply would be similarly affectionate.

Alric's head whipped around, green eyes narrowed. In the half-darkness, the bright copper streaks in his pelt were gone, replaced by ripples of sleek black. He opened his mouth to taste the air, teeth glowing silver-orange in the light of the rising moon and setting sun.

Mala stepped from the dust onto the grass, little green blades pricking her still pink and tender paw pads. Something was wrong. Alric's eyes had hardened to stone, an accusation that cut into her pelt like a thorn.

Warily, she approached her father, one cautious step at a time.

Then Alric snarled, the shadows bunching around him, teeth bared and as sharp as blades.

Rejected, Mala backed away until she was at the bottom of the hill, claws ripping through the grass. She turned and dashed back to her spot at the edge of the forest.

Mala had known she was different from the moment

she had come out of the den. Her mother had watched her more closely than her siblings, and her packmates had acted unsure of her. It hadn't seemed that important until now. Until now, when all she had felt from her packmates had been concentrated into one accusatory glance.

Why did her own father despise her?

Mala turned and started walking into the forest. Perhaps it would hold some answers for her.

A familiar growl stopped her in her tracks. She turned to see that Lora had opened one eye and was watching her. Mala flattened her ears and whimpered, asking for forgiveness. Her mother replied with a yawn.

The little black pup returned to her exploring. She understood she wasn't supposed to go into the forest or stray too far from the den, but she was a curious pup, and she needed to know what made her different from her siblings. She would risk her life for the answer she sought, to be an accepted member of the pack she had been born into.

Lora was now fully awake and watching her. Mala decided to stay by the den for now.

She sniffed each tuft of grass with the utmost precision. She scratched at the ground near the den's entrance, digging for clues. But she found nothing.

Deep down, Mala knew she wouldn't find what she was looking for by digging holes or sniffing grass. She just didn't know what else to do.

She was heading back toward her siblings, ready to take a long nap, when she noticed a mouse nosing around by the stream, warm and appetizing. She darted after it, paws slipping down the gentle slope to the water. She was only a few feet away when her leg got caught on a tree root. She tripped, sliding down the bank and whimpering as her front paws slid into the stream and were immersed in frigid water that tugged at her fur.

The stream could be dangerous for a pup as small as Mala, but Lora, tired after wresting with her pups, had fallen back asleep. There would be no wolf to save the pure black female if she fell in.

Mala stared down at the stream, enchanted by it. The water rippled like ribbons, and moonlight danced atop the ripples and sparkled in Mala's eyes. Willow trees stood on either side of the pup, their fronds dragging lazily in the current.

She lifted her paws out of the shimmering grayness, letting the cold water drip onto the grass. Gingerly, she dipped her paw in again, enjoying the icy shoots of feeling that dashed up her leg.

Mala looked down into the stream, where the water curled like liquid moon-glass around a jutting rock in the bank and pooled to stillness. She saw a pup there, lit by the last light of the sun, pelt speckled with stars.

It was a pup with pure black fur that seemed even darker in the long shadows cast by the willow trees. Orange eyes smoldered within deep-set sockets, and water dripped from a sleek-furred front paw into the pool, scattering waves across its surface.

This pup looked nothing like her siblings or any of the other wolves in the pack. It was too dark, its muzzle too angled, its body too lithe. Its ears had already risen off the top of its head, and the folds within its fur were blacker than death itself.

Mala took a nervous step back, tail between her legs, and flinched when the pup in the stream copied her movements. Mustering her courage, she swatted at the pup. A matching black paw rose up to meet hers. The water broke into ripples, and the image quivered, black and rust-orange melting into one other. Mala was looking at herself.

And now she understood why she was different.

Black Magic

Chapter 6

Two more weeks went by. The days became hotter, and the pack grew hungry. With Lora stuck at the den site and Alric absorbed in worrying about Mala, hunt after hunt failed.

Hawk crossed the stream at dusk, Wyanet a few steps behind him. A steady wind drove through the hunting ground, augmenting the whistles and chirps of the elk herd up ahead and the drumming of hooves against grass. The sky above the tree line glowed a deep orange, the last farewell of the sunset, which bled upwards into a vast gray sky twinkling with emerging stars.

Hawk slowed his gait as he neared the herd, trying to keep his breathing light and his pawsteps quiet. Wyanet stepped up beside him, eyes shining slightly in the half-darkness. He would rather have left her back at the den site, but Alric and Rynna were busy patrolling the territory, and it would have been nearly impossible to kill an adult elk on his own. He waved his tail, a signal to split up, and the two wolves forged paths in opposite directions along the outskirts of the herd.

The elks' birthing season had just begun, and the high-pitched mews of several newborns were intermixed with the calls of full-grown cow elk. Hawk broke into a trot when he caught the scent of a nearby calf on the wind. The calf huddled by her mother's side at the edge of the herd, the telltale white spots on her flank reflecting the faint starlight. Hawk licked his lips. If he could separate the calf from her mother, she would be an easy meal. He glanced over at Wyanet, prowling on the opposite side of the hunting ground, but decided against involving her. He was strong enough to make this kill all on his own. The subordinate would only get in his way … and besides, he didn't want to share credit for feeding the pack.

Hawk exploded out of his energy-conserving trot into a sprint. He barreled towards the herd, eyes watering as the cool evening air buffeted his face. A few of the elk let out low, huffing sounds of alarm, and the herd scattered, bumping into each other in their haste to get away.

Hawk slowed down a little, keeping pace with the elk without wasting strength. He began trying to isolate his target. The calf stayed by her mother's side at first, but her spindly, clumsy legs couldn't keep up for long. She dropped farther and farther behind the others and closer to Hawk's waiting teeth. He sped up again, breath coming in short, frantic pants. The elk's eyes, round and fearful on the sides of her head, spotted him as he neared her hind legs. She swerved to the side, attempting to evade him, but this only served to move her farther from the relative safety of the herd.

Hawk was awfully close now, close enough to hear the calf's rapid breathing and feel the vibrations of her hooves through the ground. A few more seconds, and she would be his prey.

An enraged screech blasted against Hawk's eardrums. Guided by reflex, he veered away from the calf, pain exploding through his shoulder as a pointed hoof rammed into it. Hawk fell sideways onto the grass, whimpering in pain, paws pummeling the ground in a vain attempt to rise. The calf's mother loomed over him, nostrils flaring as she lined up another strike. He had avoided the full impact of her first blow, but this time there was no escape. One direct hit by an elk's hooves could be enough to break bone.

Hawk's instincts took over. Magic rushed through him, sparks leaking from his eyes and flowing in golden rivulets through his fur. His powers cut through the dusk like a beacon, dulling his pain and imbuing him with speed and strength. The elk shied backwards, startled, giving Hawk enough time to stand.

Wyanet arrived, a blur of pale fur and shining teeth, charging down the mother elk. The elk's startled shriek mingled with the rush of the wind, and she galloped back towards her herd, Wyanet close behind. Under the partially clouded sky, the wolf's silvery-white fur seemed to flicker with the light of the stars, a gleaming blade whirling through the night.

Hawk took one shaky step back, then another. His magic had already ebbed away, but it had made his pelt light up like a flame in the darkness, however briefly; there was no chance Wyanet hadn't seen it. His instincts had gotten the better of him, exposing his deadly secret. He had no choice now but to run—run or risk Alric's fury when he found out what Wyanet had seen. His magic was more than a match for one cow elk, but he wasn't sure it could fend off his entire pack.

He bowed his head and turned towards the forest, gathering up the strength to flee. All his hard work, all his carefully laid plans of usurping Alric, undone by one moment of hubris. He shouldn't have taken on the calf alone, and now he was paying the price.

But then Wyanet stepped in front of him, her face calm and guarded, like a pond coated in a thin layer of ice. Her eyes were a cloudy blue-gray, and there was something knowing in the depths of her stare that froze him in his tracks.

Hawk's fur stood on end, and he stared at her with suspicion in his gaze. He and Wyanet had never been friends. Both of them were outsiders, loners who had joined the pack instead of being born into it. They were used to making their own way. Their relationship was forged from mistrust—

Hawk had fought Wyanet to earn his place in the pack. But now she stood before him, an offer at the front of her mind. She would keep his powers a secret, and he would owe her a favor in return.

It felt like a trap. Hawk glanced between Wyanet and the trees behind her. He could run now and untangle himself from this strange web. But that would mean forsaking all the promises he had made to himself and to the ancestors, vows of a leadership forged in violence. His dreams of overthrowing Alric, of become the alpha, had to be fulfilled. And perhaps Wyanet would help him along the way.

As the last rays of sunlight slipped beneath the horizon, the two wolves returned to the den site side by side. Hawk kept his head down, lost in his thoughts, occasionally glancing at his companion as she stared up at the stars with an unreadable expression on her face.

He would have to keep guard up. Wyanet might seem like just another harmless subordinate, but she had plans of her own.

Chapter 7

On a bright morning, while Alric and the rest of the pack hunted, Lora lay just outside the den with her pups scampering around her.

Ice Eyes and Greatpaw were having a staring contest near the stream. Their eyes were locked, their fur bristling. Neither could afford to look away from the other's angry glare. To do so would be a sign of submission.

Though these games might seem trivial to an outsider, they were crucial for determining each pup's place in the pack. The pups who asserted themselves over their siblings now would have a higher position in the hierarchy later on. A higher rank meant more food, warmer sleeping spots, and the respect of other wolves. The pups knew the stakes, and they each did their best to surpass the others.

Ice Eyes had quickly become the most dominant of the pups despite her small size, a fact which frustrated Alric to no end. The alpha male had encouraged Greatpaw to defeat his sister, but there was little the pup could do to overcome

Ice Eyes's strong personality. Greatpaw just didn't have the fortitude to surpass her in dominance, despite his size and strength. And Alric was too stubborn to admit that Ice Eyes would be a more natural heir, Old Way or no Old Way.

Lora exhaled, the force of her breath throwing tiny spirals of dust into the air around her head. Sometimes it seemed like the Old Way was the cause of most of their problems. It twisted the structure of the pack into something unnatural. But that was the way it had always been, and Lora didn't have the authority to change it.

After a few moments, Greatpaw and Ice Eyes grew bored of the staring contest. Ice Eyes noticed Star and Mala dozing in a circle of sunlight, extra playmates for their next game. She yipped excitedly at Greatpaw.

The two pups dashed up to their sleeping siblings and prodded them awake. Star and Mala blinked sleepily as Ice Eyes subtly communicated her idea for a game. Lora tilted her head at them, wondering what they were planning.

Her heart sank as all four of them looked at her.

Ice Eyes coordinated the attack, conveying the plan to her siblings with tail signals. As usual, she barely paused while she imparted her strategy, not giving the other pups any time to express their own ideas. Lora narrowed her eyes but didn't intervene. Ice Eyes was young. She didn't understand what being a leader meant yet; she was overcompensating for her father's attempted suppression of her dominance. Lora understood this and wondered if Alric did too.

Of course, Lora knew most of the pups' plan. They hadn't yet grasped the meaning of a surprise attack.

As Lora braced herself for the assault, she noticed the disappointed look on Star's face. Ice Eyes had made him be the diversion. Again. Star didn't really like his job, but he would allow his sister to force him into it, especially if he believed it would benefit the group.

Just this once, Lora decided to intervene. Star was such a sweet little pup ... he should be able to do what *he* wanted sometimes. She yapped at Ice Eyes, requesting that the little female allow her brother to play a different role in the attack.

Ice Eyes bared her teeth, but reluctantly agreed. A grin spread across Star's face as he stood beside his siblings as part of the attack force, and Lora's tail thumped against the ground.

Once Ice Eyes's plan had been successfully executed, the pups collapsed beside their mother, pressing against her side. She licked each one on the ears and head, smoothing down their fur. Then she whimpered gently. Wolves used whimpers and whines in many different situations, signaling fear, curiosity, or happiness depending on the context. In this case, Lora was telling her pups that everything was well, and that they were safe.

The pups wagged their little tails and snuggled closer to their mother. Greatpaw and Ice Eyes fought over a spot next to Lora's warm flank. Greatpaw used his superior size to shove his sister out of the way, but she just wiggled dexterously between him and Lora, whining happily. Star huddled as close to his mother as he could get, fearful of the world around him. Mala sat a distance away, staring off at the forest with big, orange eyes full of wonder. It had become a habit of hers to explore faraway places in her mind while her body remained trapped at the den site. Deep in the woods of her imagination, she could escape the fear and suspicion that ignited in the eyes of her packmates whenever they looked at her.

Greatpaw pressed closer to Ice Eyes, his sister's soft puppy fur tickling his nose. Ice Eyes turned and licked him on the ear, whining happily from her place right next to Lora.

For a moment, Greatpaw lay there contentedly, his affection for Ice Eyes and the rest of his family flowing through him. Then he realized what he was doing and growled softly. By leading the attack, Ice Eyes had strengthened her position as the most dominant pup and put Greatpaw at a disadvantage. He needed to strike back now and prove he wouldn't submit so easily.

Greatpaw had felt this weight on his mind since the moment he'd been named. Alric had stood over him, bright eyes staring down from a face rimmed in copper fur. There was so much expectation in that stare ... Greatpaw had taken a step back. Through the intuitive mental communication that existed between all wolves, he'd become aware of his position as Alric's heir, responsible for carrying on his father's legacy. Leadership of the Willow River pack had passed from father to son for generations, and soon it would be Greatpaw's turn to guide the pack and preserve the Old Way.

Greatpaw understood something of the Old Way and the ancestors already, just by perceiving the thoughts and emotions of his packmates. He knew what they needed from him, and he was willing to fulfill their expectations. He would rather defeat Ice Eyes honorably, without any hatred or real violence between them. Tearing his family apart for destiny and duty's sake would be wrong. Yet Ice Eyes continued to challenge him by exerting her dominance. His fair tactics weren't working. Something had to be done. He needed to be the strongest and most dominant pup, even if it meant fighting his siblings.

Greatpaw squirmed away from the warmth of Ice Eyes's fur and batted at her with giant puppy paws. Ice Eyes swatted Greatpaw in retaliation, her paw a flash of silver as it darted through the air and her piercing blue eyes hardening and sharpening to thorny rage. Greatpaw shrank back, surprised by her sudden fury, and the battle was over before it had even begun.

But the damage was done. Ice Eyes's fur stood on end. Star pressed closer to his mother. Lora stared at her pups in surprise—serious fights over dominance were rare in pups this age. Greatpaw ducked his head, shame prickling his fur. A moment ago, they had all been happy and at peace. And Greatpaw had ruined it.

Only Mala seemed unperturbed. Her gaze never left the forest, and she seemed not to have noticed what was happening.

Lora licked one paw thoughtfully, then lowered her head and closed her eyes. The pups were calm now. She wouldn't punish Greatpaw. After all, he was just doing what Alric wanted.

Lora swept the pups closer to her. She hooked a paw around Mala and drew her in as well, ignoring her daughter's whine of protest. If Mala didn't want to be an outcast, she had to stop acting like one. Then Lora closed her eyes and breathed in the warm, sweet scent of pups. It was good to be a mother.

Water splashed somewhere nearby, cutting over the babbling of the stream. Lora lifted her head and grinned as she spotted her packmates wading through the shallow current towards the den site. She stood, leaving her pups sleeping together in front of the den, and trotted up to the other wolves. The pups were still well within her line of sight, and she was close enough to make it back to them at the first scent of a bear or coyote that might want to harm them. Confident that her offspring would be safe, she touched noses with her returning packmates, tail wagging.

Lora could see the disappointment hidden behind their eyes. Another hunt, unsuccessful. And while most attempts at catching elk ended this way, it still sent a stab of worry through Lora's heart. She was the best hunter in the pack, despite her age and declining strength, but she was stuck at the den, looking after her pups. Without their alpha female leading the hunt, the Willow River pack was almost always hungry.

Lora turned to look back at her pups. She had already delayed this for too long. It was time to choose a pup sitter, a wolf to watch over her offspring while she hunted with the rest of the pack.

Her packmates sensed her intentions. Hawk, Wyanet, and Rynna stepped forward, standing in front of Lora with heads tilted expectantly. Alric took a step back and sat down to wait for his mate's decision.

Lora looked over each wolf. Hawk's face was twisted into a glare. Though the role of pup sitter was considered an honor for most wolves, a strong and dominant hunter like Hawk would never accept it. Wyanet stared down at her dainty white paws, face unreadable. She might do ... but her motives were always unclear. Lora could never fully trust her.

That left Rynna. Timid, clumsy little Rynna, her eldest daughter, who had never been able to handle much responsibility. But at least she was looking Lora in the eye.

With a sigh, Lora made her decision.

Rynna held her wagging tail low to the ground and whined with happiness, licking her mother's chin in joyful deference. She was ready to prove herself.

Rynna knew what the other adults thought of her. Most of them believed she was a clumsy, irresponsible coward and a bad choice to watch over Lora's precious litter. But despite her timidity, she was determined to rise to the challenge. She would not allow her younger siblings to suffer the same fate her brothers had.

Chapter 8

Darkness had begun to settle over the wide stretch of grass where three wolves stalked a lone cow elk.

Lora had remained with Rynna minding the pups at den site. It would be a few days before Rynna was ready to look after the pups alone. Alric led the hunt, grass tickling his paws as he ghosted towards the old, sickly elk. He could sense Hawk and Wyanet on either side of him. They had been surveying the Willow River pack's eastern border for two days, loping for hours at a time through long sections of contested territory. Such extended bursts of activity took energy, and when they had encountered a weakened cow elk left behind by her herd, they were unable to resist.

Alric tilted his head and twitched his tail, sending silent signals to his packmates as he planned out the attack. The elk stood in the center of the large expanse of grass, far from the trees. Soon, she would spot the wolves stalking towards her and run for the forest, where she could easily lose them within the dense foliage. They would have to catch her before she made it there.

The elk's fur was disheveled and matted with burrs, and her eyes were glassy. When they had the choice, wolves took only weak, sick elk, and the calves least likely to survive to adulthood. In fact, hunting this way benefitted the elk herd overall by keeping their population balanced. There was no need for shame or sadness when wolves made a kill. They hunted for their survival and that of their young.

Alric took another slow, silent step, then sprang forward and charged across the grass, his packmates behind him. The sickly cow, her eyes wide with terror, dashed away from the wolves in her prancing and unsteady gait.

Alric remained in the lead. Hawk and Wyanet ran at the back of the small group, waiting to help Alric subdue the elk in its final moments. Hawk growled in frustration, wishing he were at the head of the pack as the alpha.

If he were leader, he would make sure the ancestors got the respect they deserved. But that wasn't his only motivation for wanting to take Alric down. Memories flashed through his mind, of jutting bones and ragged fur, a flash of teeth.

Hawk pushed the painful memories away, instead imagining what it would be like to lead the pack on a hunt. How invincible Alric must have felt, running alone at the front with no wolf's steps to follow, the wind buffeting his face.

But Alric didn't feel invincible. He felt responsible. It was his duty to risk his life for his pack. Alric had to run behind the elk's flailing hooves, grab a kicking back leg in his jaws, and hold on until his prey exhausted herself. It was dangerous work, and something that Lora had become adept at over the years. Alric was less experienced, but there was no shirking his responsibility.

He had so many responsibilities. Responsibilities to his pack, to his ancestors, and to his family. So many that they had become jumbled and contradictory, scavenger birds fighting over Alric's loyalty like it was a scrap of meat. He knew a wolf like Hawk would have no problem making the choice that had been weighing heavily on Alric's mind for days. If Hawk were leader, he would put the ancestors before everything else. He would kill Mala without hesitation. But Alric wasn't Hawk.

Alric was inches away from his target. The elk's hoof suddenly flashed back at him as she kicked, and he was forced to dart away. He hung back, nervous of giving her a second chance to hurt him.

Hawk was at the back of the hunt, watching as the alpha male seemed to hesitate. The hunt was nearing the edge of the field. If the elk reached the forest, their meal would be gone, and there was no telling when they would all eat again. Now Alric, in his wariness of being kicked, was running too slowly to stop her.

If Hawk could pass the leader and take down the elk on his own, then he would claim command not just of the hunt but potentially of the pack itself. But he was too far away to catch up in time. Unless he had something to help him along.

Just before the elk reached the tree line, golden lights burst to life on Hawk's fur, like fireflies in a dark night sky. In a surge of unnatural speed and strength, he covered half the distance between himself and the Willow River leader in three gigantic bounds. Before Alric noticed his use of magic, Hawk allowed the surge of power to recede, the sparks in his fur dying out.

Alric noticed Hawk catching up to him out of the corner

of his eye. Suddenly, the alpha's hesitance vanished. He accelerated, pushing out of his energy conserving run to a full-on gallop.

The elk's eyes were wide and glassy, like the surface of a still lake, as Alric seized her back leg in his teeth. Her bones fractured in his grip. She stumbled, and her headlong dash ended as she struggled to remain on her feet. Then another set of teeth gripped her neck. With his earlier insubordination stamped out, Hawk helped Alric bring the elk down.

Wyanet ran forward, grabbed the other back leg of the elk, and pulled downwards. The three wolves heaved with all their might, jaws straining, paws sliding against the slippery grass. The cow elk staggered, then crashed to the ground, the wolves dancing back to avoid being crushed beneath her.

Alric howled with his low voice in celebration, and Wyanet joined him. Hawk did not. His muzzle was already coated in blood, staining it a strange reddish black, and his teeth were bared back in a snarl. His attempt to usurp the leader had only served to make Alric even more suspicious of his beta. At least Hawk's magic remained a secret between himself and Wyanet. He might yet have another chance to usurp Alric.

The elk's body lay at the edge of the field, surrounded by grass uprooted by the struggle. The reddish brown of its short fur was masked by the darkening sky. The alpha male presided over the carcass, forbidding the others from eating until he had taken his fill. Hawk moved forward, whining, but Alric stopped him with a step forward and a raised tail. Usually the beta would be allowed to eat before the subordinates, but not today. Not after Hawk had tried to take leadership over the hunt.

As Hawk crouched beside Wyanet to eat, shame crawled through his pelt. He had worked hard for his rank. He deserved better than this.

Someday, he vowed, Alric would regret making him an enemy. He just needed time to gain strength and to secure allies. Wyanet might seem compliant, but Hawk suspected that she didn't really approve of Alric's leadership. She had already agreed to keep Hawk's magic a secret, for reasons he couldn't quite decipher. If he could get her on his side, he would have the support necessary to keep the pack in line after he overthrew Alric. He raised his head and turned towards the alpha male, his blood-coated muzzle contorted into a snarl.

But Alric wasn't looking back at Hawk. He stared at the trees, nose twitching and teeth bared. Something was out there.

Nervously, Hawk sniffed the air. There was a sharp scent on the breeze, the scent of a rival group of wolves. He closed his eyes for a second, remembering how this smell used to nestle in his own fur. The Mud Lake pack, Hawk's birth pack, was nearby.

Alric glanced sideways at his beta, sensing the dark-furred male's discomfort. He, too, had grown uneasy. They were within the area where the Willow River pack and Mud Lake pack territories overlapped. Whenever two packs inhabited an area, an encounter was likely, maybe even a fight.

The three Willow River wolves stood around their kill, their heads raised and their ears pushed forward, waiting.

Hawk picked up more scents and growled deep in his throat. His older sister, Thorn, was leading the group. Her mate was with her, and three other wolves accompanied the alpha pair. Alric's pack was outnumbered, and the Mud Lake wolves were coming straight towards them.

The scent of these very woods lay heavily on the fur of the Mud Lake wolves. They'd been hunting here often. This made Hawk's fur bristle with indignation. He could see them now, moving like wraiths along the edge of the forest, mostly obscured by the tall grass. They were after the Willow River pack's kill.

Hawk howled a bold warning, telling them to come no further. Alric and Wyanet joined in, reinforcing the message, their howls echoing loudly through the forest. For a moment, the crickets stopped chirping.

The Mud Lake wolves ignored the howl and moved

forward. Soon, they were close enough for Hawk to see the white puffs of breath that rose from their parted jaws into the cool night air.

Thorn was at the front of the group. Her black fur stood on end, and her deep-set golden eyes glimmered above her bared teeth. She was nearly identical to Hawk, right down to the small patch of white on her chest. As the siblings' gazes met, they both flinched, and their snarls intensified.

Then Thorn looked away from her brother, turning her stare towards Alric. It was the enemy pack's leader, not its beta, who she had to intimidate if she meant to claim the elk carcass.

Hawk glanced at Alric and was unsurprised to see hatred in his eyes. The alpha male had every reason to despise Thorn. She was a female leader, dominant over even her mate. The Mud Lake pack had followed the New Way ever since she had overthrown her own father. Hawk had been barely more than a pup at the time, powerless to stop her. He could still recall the cold prickle of her teeth on his skin, punishment for even the smallest act of disobedience.

Thorn's version of the New Way was even more distorted than most. She'd not only cast aside the sacred laws of the ancestors, but had also instated herself as absolute leader, with no code or higher power to guide her. Even with his gifts, Hawk had been powerless against her. Every time he made the smallest misstep, she'd hurt his beloved sister Lily, knowing that he would do anything to keep his weaker littermate from suffering.

After many seasons, Hawk had finally found the courage to leave the pack. He had joined Willow River hoping that Lily could soon accompany him, that Alric would tolerate her weak, sickly constitution if Hawk was a strong and loyal enough beta. How wrong he had been.

Now, Hawk watched the encounter between his older sister and Alric with narrowed eyes. Both leaders viewed this as just another dispute over borders and prey. They had no idea that they were inextricably linked in Hawk's memory as wolves who had caused the most painful moment of Hawk's life. He blinked, struggling to push the thought away, to the back of his mind. He needed to focus.

The two packs stood in darkness beneath the new moon, surrounded by tall grass. It whispered and danced in the wind, pulling Hawk back to another moonless night. A season after he had joined the Willow River pack, when he and Lily had stood here, waiting.

He fought the memory, but it was no use. He was forced to relive it.

He had been standing in the field with his sister. He could remember the way Lily's dark fur hung off her like a wet rag, exposing jutting ribs outlined in shadow. She had seemed so small, so breakable. Or perhaps she had already been broken. Her eyes were full of desperation. Hawk needed to help her. She wouldn't survive out here, all alone.

Not all wolves were meant to leave their packs and start their own families. Lily couldn't survive as a lone wolf. She had been frightened of the shadows and the darkness, frightened of the pounding of elk hooves during the hunt, frightened especially of her own sister. Since the beginning, Hawk had been her protector, and she'd been devoted to him. Their bond had been the only thing sustaining Hawk while Thorn was in control.

After Hawk had left his family and fought for a position among the Willow River pack, he and Lily had often snuck away from their respective packs to meet at the border. When Thorn found out, Lily was banished.

Hawk had known how weak they both seemed, he and Lily. He had howled for his pack to come quickly. Alric had arrived before the rest of the pack, and he fixed his new beta Hawk with a quizzical stare. Then he looked at Lily, head tilted.

Hawk had watched his leader's eyes widen as he smelled Willow River elk on the half-starved female. With Hawk standing guard, she had been sneaking over the border, eating off their kills. Alric growled, his silhouette dark and menacing as he glanced between the siblings.

Hawk shrank back. He had been careless. In his desperation to secure her a position in his pack, he had forgotten to disguise the scent of Willow River prey on Lily's fur. And now they would both pay the price.

But maybe Alric would understand. Hawk had tried to convey that lone wolves needed to eat, especially half-starved ones like Lily. He had silently implored the leader to be merciful towards his sister. Perhaps her weakness would slow the Willow River pack down for a time, but with ample food and rest she could eventually grow strong.

When Alric took another step forward, towards Lily, the look in his eyes had dashed all of Hawk's hopes.

Time seemed to slow as Hawk watched Alric's claws arcing down. He had leapt forward, preparing to summon the power within himself, but he wasn't fast enough.

When Hawk had joined the Willow River pack, he had thought the Old Way would help him serve the ancestors and bring purpose to his existence. But with the Old Way's never-ending hunger to stamp out weakness, all it had done was tear Hawk's life apart. In his adherence to the old teachings, Alric had killed the one wolf Hawk cared about.

Alric had known Lily was Hawk's sister. And after he had brutally betrayed his own beta, he led the pack back to the den site as though nothing had happened. Had he thought Hawk was so devoted to the Old Way and the ancestors that he would forgive the leader for his sister's murder?

Hawk would always remain the ancestors' most dedicated servant, but he refused to believe that this was what they wanted. And any respect he had felt for the Old Way had been snuffed out along with Lily's life.

Who did Alric think he was, to deem any wolf useless, to believe their existence was pointless just because they seemed weak? Hawk's sister hadn't been pointless. Hawk had needed her. She had been the only thing stopping him from being utterly alone. With her gone, there was nothing to stop him from succumbing to the darkness of grief, rage, and revenge.

Even before Lily's death, Hawk had longed to overthrow Alric. Sometimes the ancestors appeared in his dreams, spectral figures of wolves, their pelts swimming with light, mentally urging him to take charge of the pack. Faithless wolves might say those were just dreams, but Hawk believed the ancestors truly meant for him to lead. Why else had they given him such powerful magic? And after Lily was murdered, Hawk became even more convinced. It was his purpose, his destiny to kill Alric and outlaw the Old Way in this pack.

Hawk narrowed his eyes and pulled himself back into the present.

The two growling, snarling packs of wolves faced off, neither of them daring to move. Alric's tail lashed, then fell, dangling by his legs. He turned and led his pack back into the trees, away from their kill.

The three Willow River wolves were not strong enough to face five adults in their prime. They would avoid this part of their territory for the next few weeks, letting the Mud Lake pack hunt here when they pleased. They would have to bring Lora or Rynna next time, or else only venture onto this land when they were sure the rival pack was nowhere nearby.

The Willow River pack needed more members. Five wolves weren't enough to defend a territory of such size, and the surrounding packs were already aware of this. It was only a matter of time before they were overrun, or one of them was killed by a rival pack member. Alric hung his head, conscious of the danger facing his pack.

Hawk walked behind him, a shadow slipping through the trees. His golden eyes were full of hatred and grief, glowing fiercely like stars brought down to earth. Soon, he would make Alric pay.

Chapter 9

Heat radiated from the smooth, stormy-gray stone that served as Wyanet's resting place, soaking up into her belly and flowing down to the tip of her tail. The sun shone down from a clear sky, burning away the last of the early morning dew.

Wyanet sat on a boulder in the center of the hunting grounds, a short walk from the den. The boulder lay within a dip in the ground, where it seemed like some giant wolf had dug out a little random hole in the center of the hunting field. A small jumble of mismatched rocks lay along the edges of the dip, and the pack sometimes came in the morning to rest on their smooth surfaces.

Wyanet was the only one here today. The rock she sat upon was perfectly smooth, a gray the color of a raincloud. She had claimed it long ago, and she thought it suited her. The most beautiful rock for the most beautiful wolf.

Lora and Rynna were back at the den with the pups. They were six weeks old now and had just started to be weaned off milk. The two females were busy eating small strips of meat from a recently killed deer and regurgitating it for the pups.

Shifting her weight to a more comfortable position, Wyanet twitched her birdsong-assailed ears. *She* should be the one with pups to raise. She had wanted to be a mother for a long as she could remember. And yet, Lora was the pack's alpha female, the pack's mother. Three years in a row, Lora had been given the chance to raise offspring. And she had failed spectacularly every time.

Even worse, she had betrayed the ancestors by keeping a cursed pup alive. Wyanet had been raised in a pack far away, but her parents had still taught her to respect the ancestors and follow the Old Way. Lora was from a family just like Wyanet's. She should know better than to put the entire pack in danger by allowing Mala to live.

Wyanet flicked her tail contemptuously, her blue-flecked eyes glimmering with envy and resentment. She was tired of being a subordinate. She wanted the respect of her packmates, the exhilaration of leading the hunt, the joy of raising pups of her own. But in a pack that followed the Old Way, only the alphas could have pups. Wyanet *needed* to be alpha female, needed it like she needed air to breathe and meat to eat.

Wyanet had spent nearly a season scheming and formulating a plan. Now, everything was going the way it should.

Over the past few weeks, she had done her best to stay

close to Alric's side. She'd wanted to prove both her strength and dominance. By next winter, Lora would be seven years old and very weak. Alric would have no choice but to accept Wyanet as his new alpha female. And by keeping Hawk's magic a secret, she had bought his support. Even if leadership changed, Wyanet would remain the most powerful female in the pack.

The sound of pebbles clacking down the side of the stony dip made Wyanet raise her head and lift one paw in surprise. Alric was standing at the top of the dip, grinning down at her. He leapt from rock to rock until he stood on the sandy floor, in front of Wyanet.

On her perch high on the rock, she was looking down at the alpha. She moved to correct her position, leaping to the ground and bowing her head to Alric. Then she looked up at him and grinned, tail wagging.

Alric grinned right back at Wyanet, so she took things one step further, dropping into a play-bow, tongue lolling. Alric's wolf-smile widened, and he growled teasingly at her, taking a sudden step forward. She darted away and ran up the side of the dip with the alpha in pursuit, pebbles raining down behind them.

All wolves loved a good game of tag. Alric chased Wyanet across the open field, the cool air tickling their ears. Wyanet leapt over a patch of tiny blue flowers, paws crashing back down onto the grass on the other side. Alric pounced after her and pinned her to the ground. After grappling for a few seconds, Alric got up and dashed away with Wyanet in pursuit.

Back and forth they went, until they collapsed in a panting heap in the middle of the meadow. Alric whined happily. He had needed to stretch his legs, and Wyanet was fun to play with. Alric suspected that she had an ulterior for being so friendly, but he was still drawn to her.

A moment later, thoughts of his pups made Alric get up and trot back towards the den, feeling a bit guilty. He should check on how Lora and Rynna were getting along.

Wyanet returned to her rock and lay down as though nothing had happened. Truthfully, she felt like grinning and howling and wagging her tail all at once. She knew Alric liked her. Now she just had to prove that she would make a better alpha female than Lora.

She would manipulate her way to becoming alpha female, and Lora would only be able to sit and watch.

Chapter 10

It was an overcast morning at the Willow River den site. The clouds swelled until they covered the whole sky, and the air grew heavy with water vapor that condensed into tiny droplets on the wolves' fur.

The pups tussled in front of the den while Lora happily watched. Their coats gleamed under the watery sunlight, and their eyes shone. All four were healthy and strong. Lora was proud of the way she was raising them. They had just finished being weaned, and their newfound independence from their mother gave them the urge to explore. It was all Lora could do to keep them near the den site. Without Rynna's help, the alpha female didn't know what she would do. Her eldest daughter had been a quick learner and was quite dedicated to keeping her younger siblings safe. Now Rynna supervised the pups as they played, intervening every now and then when one of them got too rough.

Alric sat on the hill above the den, watching his offspring play with narrowed eyes. He glanced at Lora, meeting her gaze for a moment, before turning his attention to Mala. Lora shivered at the hatred in his stare. Alric had wanted to do something about Mala since the moment she'd emerged from the den. But he was reluctantly biding his time, waiting for Lora to let down her guard so she wouldn't be there to challenge him.

Lora lowered her head and stared at the ground. She wasn't sure how to respond. She cared equally about both Alric and Mala, and the thought of choosing between them was too much for her to bear. She couldn't look at Alric without worrying, now. But surely, he would never truly harm Mala. Lora still had hope that she wouldn't need to fight him in the end. Perhaps Mala would eventually prove her worth to her father. Having such a wolf on their side would make the Willow River pack look strong. Other packs would be too afraid to trespass on Willow River territory if they believed it was defended by dark magic.

A harsh whine from somewhere nearby cut through Lora's thoughts. Greatpaw had Star pinned to the ground, both their coats covered in scraps of dirt and leaves. Star's eyes were wide, his little paws kicking feebly, but he couldn't shake his brother off. The large pup batted eagerly at his smaller brother with hard paw-strikes, oblivious to how much he was hurting Star.

Rynna darted forward, her paws sliding on bare, damp

ground. She scooped up Greatpaw in her teeth in spite of his whimpers of protest and held him gently by the scruff of his neck, carrying him a few feet away from his brother. Then she set him down, ignoring Alric's growl of frustration.

Alric wanted his pups to fight their own battles, to become strong so they could serve the pack well when they grew older. He didn't mind Greatpaw, the presumed future leader of the pack, showing dominance over his siblings. But Lora felt the pups' happiness should come before duty, at least for now. She moved to stand beside Rynna and growled at Greatpaw, sending him a firm message to be more careful in the future. Then she turned and trotted over to Star, licking the top of his head and sniffing him thoroughly to make sure he wasn't hurt. After a moment, Greatpaw joined her with a remorseful expression on his face and whined at his brother in apology. Star stood up and wagged his tail, and all was forgiven.

Alric narrowed his eyes. Lora could sense his mounting frustration. There was a sharper quality to everything around them, like Alric was willing the air particles themselves to dig like pine needles into Lora's skin. She didn't know what to do about it, so she curled up in front of the den and buried her nose in her paws.

Ice Eyes saw her opportunity. While her mother was distracted, she yipped at the two males, who instantly broke apart. Quiet, clever Mala saw what her sister was planning and trotted over with her tail wagging, eager for the first time to join in. Finally, her siblings were going to explore the forest, as Mala had always longed to do.

Ice Eyes, Greatpaw, and Mala dashed away from the den, delighted with their opportunity to investigate. Hesitant Star stayed behind. He was afraid of what lay beyond his mother's protective gaze. He curled up between her two front paws, yawning.

Star knew that the other pups might be walking straight into danger. He thought about accompanying them. Maybe he could watch their backs and try to keep them out of even worse trouble. But fear won out, and he pressed closer to his mother, feeling guilty. Afraid his siblings would be angry with him for spoiling their fun, he didn't communicate the danger to Lora.

Lora grinned as she felt her son's warm fur tickle her paws, but she was oblivious to the other pups' absence. She was lost in her thoughts.

Alric, however, did notice. He stood and followed the pups towards the forest, slipping into the trees and moving through the underbrush, silent as a leaf drifting on the wind.

The three little explorers trotted through the woods. Ice Eyes pranced confidently at the front of the group. Greatpaw more than matched her excitement, zigzagging back and forth in her wake. Mala lagged behind, investigating each new plant or scent trail with curiosity.

One smell in particular caught her attention. It was a dark, musty odor that hit Mala's nose like a solid wall. Something about it made her want to turn and run.

Yipping fearfully at the other two pups, she turned around to dash back to the den.

And came face to face with a gigantic, dark brown bear.

Mala had to crane her neck to see all of it. Its face was something like a wolf's, but rounder and with a tan muzzle. And bigger. Much bigger. It stood on its hind legs, its ungroomed fur hanging in clumps from its belly, trampling ferns under its massive back paws. Its mouth hung open, exposing a row of sharp yellow teeth. All of this Mala observed with eyes as wide as acorns.

The female grizzly bear had smelled the three pups, alone in the woods, and had come to collect an easy meal. She had approached from downwind, so they had only scented her at the last moment. Now she was ready to collect her bounty. She would show no mercy. She had her own cub to feed.

The pups stared up at the bear, frozen. They were trapped up against a wide tree trunk with nowhere to run.

The bear raised her paw and prepared to slam it down on Mala.

Then Alric bounded out of the trees. His steps were silent, but he growled to announce his arrival. Now it was the bear's turn to freeze in place, wobbling on her hind legs as the pups looked between her and their father.

Alric calmly approached Ice Eyes and Greatpaw and stood between them and the bear. They cowered behind their father, shivering. Then Greatpaw whined at Mala, who stood outside Alric's protection.

Mala stared at Alric, pleading with her eyes. But he turned away and walked back into the woods, lifting Ice Eyes by the scruff of her neck and hurrying Greatpaw along in front of him.

Mala's last protection faded into the trees, its only farewell the last crunch of a leaf under paw.

Alric felt like he was being torn in two. By abandoning Mala, he was following the path the ancestors had put before him. He was also tearing his own family apart. While it may be his duty to let Mala die, his instincts as a father were to defend his pups to the death. With every step he took, his pain intensified. But he didn't let himself look back.

The bear had no knowledge of Alric's hesitancy. Her cub was hungry. She dropped down onto four legs and again drew back her paw, ready to end the little life in front of her. In the split second before Mala was ripped apart, she begged the ancestors not to let her die.

Then two great weights slammed into the bear's side, throwing her claws off course. The bear wheeled around as fast as her thick legs would allow and found herself staring into two pairs of eyes, one yellow and one green. A duo of nearly identical female wolves stood before her, baring their teeth.

The pup's family had returned. The bear wouldn't risk going up against an angry she-wolf protecting her pup, much less *two* angry she-wolves. She lumbered away into the trees.

Lora and Rynna converged on Mala, covering the pup with licks and pressing their bodies against hers. Because Star had overcome his cowardice and finally alerted Lora to the danger, Mala was alive. Had he waited a moment more, she would be food in the bear's belly by now.

The alpha female felt guilty for not paying attention, but there was no way to change that now. At least Mala was safe.

Lora howled, calling desperately for Ice Eyes and Greatpaw. Alric responded in a reassuring tone. They were safe with him.

Lora sighed in relief and started walking back to the den with her two daughters beside her. Alric must have accidentally left Mala behind.

But there was a worm of doubt at the back of her mind, and she couldn't help feeling uneasy. What if Mala could never truly be safe, even within her own pack?

Black Magic

Chapter 11

The kill that day was an easy one. An old, sickly bull elk had lain near the edge of the herd, his eyes dull and glassy. The hunters had encircled him, closing in until his courage gave out and he ran. Then they had chased him down, Lora striking the final blow to his neck. Now the pack was gathered around the fresh carcass, sides heaving from the chase.

Summer was almost here, and the pups were seven weeks old. Soon, the pack would take them to the summer home, where they would live and grow and learn until autumn's arrival. Pups and adults alike could leave to explore the surrounding woods, but they would always return to the clearing where the pack camped out during the hottest days of the year.

The journey was long and tiring for pups so young. The adults had to hunt more than usual so the pups could eat and grow stronger.

Wind buffeted their fur as they stood around the kill, and cool air pricked the skin beneath their thick coats. The sun was obscured by dense, dark clouds, and the pack danced around the carcass eagerly, desperate to eat before it started to rain. A thin rope of drool dropped slowly from the corner of Hawk's mouth, like a string lowering a spider to the ground.

Alric sensed his packmates' impatience. He raised his head and howled, his long, low note riding the wind all the way back to the den site where Rynna guarded the pups. Hearing it, Rynna grinned and licked her lips, ears swatting at the flies that buzzed around her head. She'd be able to feed on what remained of the elk once the hunters returned.

Meanwhile, Alric stepped up to the carcass. Slowly, he lowered his head and sank his teeth into the kill, breaking through the elk's tough skin to tear away a choice strip of meat.

He let no other wolf approach, not even his mate, until he had devoured the most nutritious portions of kill. The liver was his favorite, and he chewed it happily while the other wolves waited. Each packmate seemed as though they were teetering on claw-tips as they watched Alric eat.

Finally, Alric grinned and lowered his tail. This was his signal for the alpha female to approach. Lora dipped her head in his direction. She took one step forward, then another … and then white flashed across her vision. Wyanet now stood in her way. The other female's tail was casually raised in dominance, a sly wolf grin stretched across her face.

Lora growled. Wyanet wouldn't get away with this. The alpha female bared her teeth, shoved her ears forward aggressively, and raised her head and neck above her rival's. For a moment, Wyanet looked afraid.

Then a strong gust of wind slammed into the pack, and frail Lora was knocked off-balance, her paws scrabbling for purchase on the grass. Wyanet's confidence returned as she witnessed her opponent's weakness. She snarled and snapped her teeth next to Lora's muzzle, the sound cracking through the open meadow, and the older female shied away. Then Wyanet moved her head above Lora's.

This was the first time Wyanet had challenged the alpha female, and she felt exhilarated but incredibly nervous. If Lora won this battle of wills, she could drive Wyanet from the pack altogether.

In hierarchy battles like this, not a drop of blood would be shed. Everything hinged on who could intimidate and dominate their opponent into acquiescing. Usually, one wolf would back down before it came to a real fight.

Alric whimpered softly, conflicted. He had been with Lora for so long that she felt like a part of him. He had wanted her as his mate for life. But he couldn't help wondering how much easier his life would be if Wyanet were the alpha female. Lora was the only thing standing between him and Mala, and he still believed Mala needed to die for the sake of the pack. At any moment, her dark powers could be unleashed upon them.

Lora reared up on her hind legs and placed her front paws on Wyanet's shoulders. Wyanet tried to shrink back, but Lora held her in place. Then she fixed the white female with an ice-cold stare. Wyanet looked away.

Lora, triumphant, ate at the carcass. A moment later, Hawk joined her. Wyanet, the lowest-ranking pack member present, ate last, her eyes lowered in shame.

Hawk watched the whole encounter impassively. It didn't matter to him who the alpha female was. His goal was defeating Alric and assuming his position as leader. He tore hungrily at the carcass, knowing it would help give him the strength he needed.

Lora noticed Hawk's greed for the elk meat. He had been eating much more than usual lately. She knew there could be only one reason: to challenge Alric.

Hawk's dark coat gleamed in the sun as he lifted his head from the carcass. He was nearly as strong as Alric now, and perhaps more determined. If his goal truly was to become leader ... Alric would have to be cautious.

Lora backed away from the carcass. Her appetite had vanished. She hadn't realized how unstable the pack truly was, with four wolves vying for power. If she lost her position as alpha female, what would that mean for her family?

Why was Wyanet trying to take Lora's rank now, just after she had given birth? During this time of year, Lora was under

Alric's protection. He wouldn't let Wyanet steal her rank.

Or would he? Wyanet's challenge was sudden, but it was also confident. There had been a glint of triumph in her eyes, as though she was certain of her victory. Could Alric have planned this, hoping that with Lora out of the way, he could finally take Mala out of the picture?

Lora stood and shook out her fur, a growl at the back of her throat. She shouldn't be thinking such things. Alric would never betray her like that.

Chapter 12

Rynna stood beside her packmates, staring out at the stream's opposite bank, legs shaking under her.

The pups huddled at her paws, gazing fearfully at the swift current. They were nine weeks old and weaned. Their adult guard hairs were growing in. Now, it was time for the pack to bring them to the summer home. And to do so, they would have to cross the stream. The pups were too small to cross on their own, and too large to be carried. Rynna knew all too well the dangers of the stream's churning waters.

The other wolves were almost as nervous. They glanced between Alric and the stream, ignoring the abundance of early summer that surrounded them. Berries clung to all the bushes, fruits hung from the branches of trees, and a herd of elk feasted fearlessly on the tall grass by the water's edge, seemingly oblivious to the wolf pack nearby. The afternoon sun shone on the tops of the trees, which had slipped out of their pale spring leaves and put on some darker attire. Alric's eyes no longer matched the foliage behind him. They stood out like bright emerald gems among the rich, dark green that was draped across the forest.

It wasn't just the land that looked different. The pups did as well. The dark brown coats of puppyhood were slowly being replaced by thicker, more colorful fur, a sign from the ancestors that the pack's journey must begin.

The other side of the stream seemed a long way away. The water raced past the pack from left to right, dodging rocks with terrifying speed. After a hard rainfall, it would bellow and roar like a bear. Luckily, it hadn't rained for several weeks, but the stream was still perilous for young pups. At least there was no wind to knock the wolves off-balance.

Alric was the first to move. He scooped up Greatpaw, holding him by the scruff of the neck. The pup's fur had turned reddish-brown, with touches of gray. His eyes were green. Alric wagged his tail, noticing how much Greatpaw resembled him, though the red pup's fur was brighter than his father's. He was almost too big to be carried, but the alpha didn't want to risk his heir being swept up by the current and drowning. He darted across the stream, Greatpaw hanging limply in his jaws. Hawk followed close behind him.

Lora carried Mala across next. She and Rynna were the only members of the pack who would get near the black pup. Unlike her siblings, Mala's fur hadn't changed a bit. She was a pure shade of black, and her eyes still burned orange. This

Chapter 12

Rynna stood beside her packmates, staring out at the stream's opposite bank, legs shaking under her.

The pups huddled at her paws, gazing fearfully at the swift current. They were nine weeks old and weaned. Their adult guard hairs were growing in. Now, it was time for the pack to bring them to the summer home. And to do so, they would have to cross the stream. The pups were too small to cross on their own, and too large to be carried. Rynna knew all too well the dangers of the stream's churning waters.

The other wolves were almost as nervous. They glanced between Alric and the stream, ignoring the abundance of early summer that surrounded them. Berries clung to all the bushes, fruits hung from the branches of trees, and a herd of elk feasted fearlessly on the tall grass by the water's edge, seemingly oblivious to the wolf pack nearby. The afternoon sun shone on the tops of the trees, which had slipped out of their pale spring leaves and put on some darker attire. Alric's eyes no longer matched the foliage behind him. They stood out like bright emerald gems among the rich, dark green that was draped across the forest.

It wasn't just the land that looked different. The pups did as well. The dark brown coats of puppyhood were slowly being replaced by thicker, more colorful fur, a sign from the ancestors that the pack's journey must begin.

The other side of the stream seemed a long way away. The water raced past the pack from left to right, dodging rocks with terrifying speed. After a hard rainfall, it would bellow and roar like a bear. Luckily, it hadn't rained for several weeks, but the stream was still perilous for young pups. At least there was no wind to knock the wolves off-balance.

Alric was the first to move. He scooped up Greatpaw, holding him by the scruff of the neck. The pup's fur had turned reddish-brown, with touches of gray. His eyes were green. Alric wagged his tail, noticing how much Greatpaw resembled him, though the red pup's fur was brighter than his father's. He was almost too big to be carried, but the alpha didn't want to risk his heir being swept up by the current and drowning. He darted across the stream, Greatpaw hanging limply in his jaws. Hawk followed close behind him.

Lora carried Mala across next. She and Rynna were the only members of the pack who would get near the black pup. Unlike her siblings, Mala's fur hadn't changed a bit. She was a pure shade of black, and her eyes still burned orange. This had upset Alric, who had taken it as proof that Mala was indeed a servant of the darkest ancestors.

But Lora wouldn't accept that Mala was any different from her siblings. She held her pup in a gentle grip and walked carefully across the stream, fur prickling with apprehension as she felt the cool water tugging on her paws. Then she set Mala down next to Alric. He flinched, but didn't move, so Lora sat on Mala's other side and grinned at her mate. She wanted him to know that she understood how he felt, but she wished he would try to see his daughter differently and accept her for who she was. There wasn't the slightest hint that she had dark magic, no evidence of her supposed evil nature, besides the way she looked.

On the opposite bank, Wyanet scooped up Ice Eyes and began to cross the stream. Ice Eyes's fur matched the water below her: silver, paler than Lora's and Rynna's, with streaks of black and gray. She had not a hint of red on her pelt, which shimmered attractively in the sunlight. She was still small, and her eyes were still the most piercing shade of pale blue.

Eager to prove herself to Alric, Wyanet crossed quickly, Ice Eyes's scruff held gently between her teeth.

Rynna was last. Her bluish paws dipped in and out of the water, testing the current. She whined softly. This was where her siblings had died. They had been playing on the stream's bank when the flash flood hit.

These four pups had already outlived Rynna's littermates by a full month. They were bigger and stronger, and they might be able to survive the rapids and swim to shore. But Rynna couldn't quite cast off her fear.

She scooped up Star. His pale fur had grown lighter in the past few weeks. Now, he was white with flecks of cream. His eyes had changed to pale yellow, like Lora's, and the diamond-shaped mark on his forehead had darkened to gray.

Rynna put one paw in the stream, then the other. The current was fast, and it threatened to sweep a wolf as small as Rynna off her feet. But she kept her balance and ran halfway across, throwing up tiny splashes where her paws landed.

She was approaching the section of the stream where the current was fastest, the water white and frothing. To Rynna's right, it flowed clear and fast straight down between two boulders. Even though it was only a three-foot drop, Star could be rammed against a boulder on the way down, hard enough to break bones.

Rynna's eyes were wide with fear. She had made this crossing by herself a hundred times before with ease, but Star was a cumbersome load. And if she dropped him, she'd never forgive herself.

Lora whined at her daughter from the other side of the stream, trying to coax her onwards. Encouraged, Rynna took one step forward, then another.

It all happened in a moment. A sharp rock cut into her paw and she yelped. Star slid out of her mouth and was enveloped by icy water. Tossed by the current, he bumped against rocks on his swift journey down the stream. Rynna lunged after him with a terrified whine, but the current was too swift, and she had no way to retrieve him. The boulders were no danger to him, at least not yet. It was the cold that threatened to end his life. Rynna had felt that same cold before, on the day her brothers had drowned. Like a thousand tiny snakes made of snow were slithering across her skin.

Star's head bobbed up and down in the water, his ears pinned back. And then he disappeared completely. It was the waterfall, carrying him downwards at a terrifying speed. Below, sharp rocks waited to break his fall. If he hit them …

Rynna prayed desperately to the ancestors to let Star live. She wouldn't be able to bear it if her little brother died in the same way her littermates had, and all because of her mistake. There were so many things still waiting for him: the journey to the summer home with his siblings, the games he would play, the hunts he would go on, the courage he would gain as he grew. Only if he survived this fall.

Rynna stared at the place where her brother had been, numb with terror. And then a sudden strong gust of wind whistled in her ears.

The pack watched as Star was hurled from the drop just

before hitting the bottom. He splashed into the deep, still pool below, his small body throwing water in all directions. Then his head went under, his tiny, churning paws unable to keep him afloat.

Lora leapt into the water, fishing her son out before the current could latch onto him again. Then she set him on the stream bank and covered his sodden fur with wolf kisses.

Rynna stood motionless as the cold water flowed over her paws, eyes wide and blank with shock. How had Star escaped? Had something broken his fall? Slowly, the tension drained out of Rynna's trembling legs and bristling fur. The ancestors had heard her prayer.

She waded out of the stream, eyes fixed on Star, barely able to believe that he was sitting safe on the grass. She approached Lora and licked her muzzle in apology. Lora whined her forgiveness. No harm had been done ... this time.

Chapter 13

After the near-disastrous crossing, Alric was wary. Star had done the impossible. He had escaped the drop uninjured. It was miraculous. But anything so out of the ordinary was suspicious to Alric, even if it had saved his son's life. No matter how much he wanted to believe that this was the ancestors' doing and not the result of dark magic, he couldn't know for certain. Perhaps Mala's abilities had manifested themselves at last. Or perhaps another wolf had powers, not evil as Mala's would be but simply neutral. Either way, the safety and order of the Willow River pack was at stake. Wolves with magic could easily seize power for themselves and disrupt the pack's natural hierarchy.

The alpha led his pack over to the rocky dip in the ground, in the center of the meadow. The grass was warm and soft under his paws, and he was reluctant to leave it for the dust and stone of the hollow. A fly buzzed around his face as he scrambled down the short slope to the bottom of the dip, then leapt onto the highest rock.

Each of the wolves clambered onto their own perches. Lora had her gray-brown boulder opposite her mate's, the color of an elk's fur. Hawk sat on a small and uncomfortable spike just below Alric, snarling with irritation. Wyanet posed proudly on her flat, slate-gray stone. And Rynna sat on the ground, beside the pups.

The pack raised their voices in song. Today's howl was filled with equal measures of fear and excitement. The wolves had overcome the obstacle of the stream crossing, but the journey to the summer home had barely begun.

Alric whined loudly, silencing the pack. It was time for another of the Willow River wolves' most important rituals. For generations, litters of pups had come here before continuing their journey to the summer home, seeking the ancestors' blessings.

Alric stared down at his pups, jolts of anxious energy flowing through his fur. What would the ancestors think when they saw his cursed daughter? For a moment, he considered skipping the ceremony, then discarded the thought with a twitch of his tail-tip. Deserting the Willow River pack's ancient customs would only make the ancestors angrier.

Alric called the pups to join him on top of the big rock, a four-foot climb from the ground. This was their test. If they weren't strong enough to make it onto the boulder, they wouldn't receive their father's favor for the journey. The first pup to reach the top gained the respect of the pack and was deemed the most likely to survive to adulthood.

Alric knew that the ancestors would send many dangers to test the Willow River pack during the journey. Star nearly drowning was only the first. By making it to the top of the rock, the pups gained not just the alpha's blessing, but also that of the ancestors. The ancient wolves in the sky would look kindly upon these pups and might spare them from hardship in the future.

The pups glanced at each other. Greatpaw took a step toward the rock, dust flowing up like mist around his legs. Ice Eyes mirrored him, head held high with resolve.

Mala and Star hung back, watching their more dominant siblings face off. They knew there was little chance of them making it to the top first. They would wait until the initial race up the boulder was finished before taking their time climbing to the summit.

Ice Eyes and Greatpaw charged towards the rock, throwing up pebbles in their wake. Greatpaw reached the stone first and leapt halfway up in two quick bounds, paws sliding against its smooth surface. He began slipping backwards down the boulder, losing half the distance he had covered, before his front claws gained purchase in a tiny crack. He hung there, back legs churning, stuck.

Ice Eyes took a more careful approach. She moved

slowly from one tiny paw hold to the next, eyes narrowed in concentration. Her sleek silver fur became caked with dust, and her head started spinning from exhaustion. It was hard work for a pup as small as she.

Alric watched the pups climb, head tilted. He was certain Greatpaw would reach the top first. The male was almost twice his sister's size, and at least thrice her strength. Surely, Ice Eyes could never beat him.

Both pups were almost to the top of the rock. Greatpaw had overcome his earlier setback and had quickly closed the distance between himself and his sister. Now, the two of them clung side by side to the boulder's surface, mere inches from the smooth, flat space where Alric stood.

They strained their paws, reaching for the top.

Ice Eyes was so close. She could feel dirt particles from the side of the rock caking on her paw pads, and the heat of the afternoon sun on her back. This was it. Her chance to prove to her family that she was worth something. She was the most dominant pup of her litter, but Alric still wouldn't make her his heir. He thought she was just a weak little female, incapable of becoming alpha. Ice Eyes knew the laws of the Old Way, knew she was forbidden from leading the pack, but why couldn't the Old Way be changed? Ice Eyes wanted to be leader more than anything else, and she was sure she'd make a better one than Greatpaw. She just needed to reach the top of the rock, needed to prove that she was just as worthy as Greatpaw to lead this pack. Almost there …

Suddenly, a shadow fell on her, and she looked up to see Alric's massive paw looming above her head, blocking her way to the rock's summit.

It was over. Greatpaw scrambled up to stand beside his father, and Alric's paw disappeared as quickly as it had arrived. Ice Eyes clawed her way to the top and collapsed on the stone, the sun's heat beating its way into her bones. Because of her father's interference, she had lost.

She and Greatpaw would have reached the top together. They would have shared the place of honor in front of the alpha male, both of them earning the ancestors' highest blessing. But no. Alric couldn't let her beat his precious heir. He couldn't even let her tie him. In his eyes and in the pack's, she would forever be second to Greatpaw.

A blinding rage swept over her. Greatpaw stood in front of Alric, not even realizing what had happened, not even noticing his sister sprawled, exhausted, in the dust. He was too wrapped up in his victory to care, and she *hated* him for it. And she hated her father, too.

The other wolves hadn't noticed, either. Or they didn't care enough to react. Lora and Rynna gazed at Greatpaw with pride, while Mala and Star were immersed in climbing up the rock.

Mala raced upwards almost as fast as Greatpaw had. Star was somewhere below her, moving at turtle speed to avoid getting hurt. Mala was stronger and faster than him, and she wanted to prove it. She didn't care about the consequences.

Mala scrambled to the top of the boulder before Star had even made it halfway. She stared up happily into the unreadable green eyes of her father. He would have to acknowledge her now. The ancestors would be furious if he broke the rules of the ceremony a second time, even for her.

Alric tilted his head at his daughter. For several seconds, he wasn't sure what course to take.

He couldn't expect the benevolent ancestors that guarded the Willow River pack to give Mala their blessing. She was a cursed pup, a servant of evil. It was unthinkable.

So, Alric nudged Mala off the boulder with one contemptuous flick of his paw. She sailed downward, flipping over in the air like a tumbleweed and landing with a thump and a whimper.

Mala scrambled to her feet after a moment, bruises but not seriously hurt. She took a step towards the rock, ready to try again. But her path was blocked by Rynna, who knew better than to test Alric's temper.

Star was halfway up the boulder. His little white paws shook from exhaustion. He was still soaking wet after his impromptu swim, and the cold water had drained much of the strength out of him. He wasn't sure if he could make it to the top.

He wasn't even sure if he *deserved* to make it. Star was the omega pup of his litter. He ate last and always allowed his siblings to beat him in play-wrestling. He knew that he should be the last to reach the boulder's summit. Yet Mala was still sitting on the dusty ground under Rynna's sharp eye, unable to do anything but sit and watch.

Star didn't like conflict. He didn't like adversity. It would be so much easier to let himself fall, to give up.

Star sighed and allowed his hold on the boulder's surface to relax.

Then he heard a sharp yip of encouragement from the ground below. Mala wanted him to make it to the top. She wouldn't let Alric's behavior ruin this for Star, too. She didn't need the blessing of the ancestors. They had never once answered her prayers, never stood in her father's way. It was through her own resilience—and with some help from her mother and siblings—that she had survived. But after Star's almost-fatal swim in the stream, it seemed like he could use the ancestors' protection. Mala didn't want him to give up for her sake.

So, Star tightened his grip and kept climbing. Every time he seemed to run out of energy and willpower, Mala would encourage him with a yap or a whine, and he would find the strength to continue.

Finally, he reached the top.

Alric howled, a sharp sound echoed by the rest of the pack. The three pups on the boulder joined in, their voices still high and thin with youth. Ice Eyes seethed with anger and righteous indignation. Greatpaw had begun to suspect why his sister was so upset, and guilt crept in around his triumph. Star stopped mid-howl and peered down at Mala, upset for her. Mala didn't howl at all. She sat silently on the ground, below all her packmates.

Lora perched on her smooth, brown rock, watching Alric howl like nothing was wrong. She wished she could growl at him, snap her teeth next to his ears until he realized the damage he was doing to his family. Yet she knew it would do no good. Alric was the alpha male. Alric presided over the ceremonies. He maintained the pack's customs.

And she cared about him. He was her mate.

But she wasn't sure if he still deserved to be.

With unease circling the pack like scavenger birds over a kill, they set off towards the summer home.

Chapter 14

Ice Eyes dragged her paws as she walked at the back of her pack, muscles aching. Her paws were so sore that the grass beneath them seemed as sharp as thorns, and the sun was as hot as she had ever felt it. The long journey to the summer home was taking a toll. She had to move her legs three times as fast as the adults to keep up, and the arduous climb up the boulder had left her tiny body exhausted before they had even started.

Greatpaw seemed to be having a much easier time. He was larger and stronger. He had the favor of the ancestors now, the blessing she had earned but never received. They would give him the strength to continue.

The pack was walking through an open field bordered by conifer trees. The soft wind picked up, ruffling Ice Eyes's fur. She twitched an ear and bristled slightly. It was unfair. So unfair that it made her stomach ache and her head hurt.

If she wanted Alric to acknowledge her, she'd have to show him, over and over again, how strong she really was.

That was when her paws collapsed under her.

She flopped to the ground with a distressed whine. Lora sprang immediately to her daughter's side, nosing her in concern. The pack gathered around Ice Eyes, flattening their ears nervously.

Alric tilted his head. The tiny female's weakness reaffirmed his confidence that Ice Eyes could never win in a fight, or lead a hunt, or make a good leader. The pack would have to wait for Ice Eyes to recover before they could continue the journey. Alric yipped loudly, commanding the other wolves to give her time.

Hawk and Wyanet sat towards the edge of the field, twitching their ears and flicking their tails with impatience. They didn't want to wait, but they would follow Alric's orders. Despite Wyanet's ambition and Hawk's thirst for revenge, both were pleased with how Alric had handled the earlier ceremony.

Lora and Rynna, however, were appalled at the alpha's actions towards his daughters. But support from her mother and sister didn't make Ice Eyes feel any better. They weren't brave enough to challenge Alric's decisions. They couldn't help her. When they approached her to see if she was well, she growled at them. They backed away, exchanging confused glances.

Alric watched this from a small rise at one end of the

clearing, his eyes narrowed. An alpha knew trouble when he saw it. The pack's loyalties were splitting.

The pups were too confused to take a side, and it wouldn't have mattered if they had. Mala and Star sat together near their exhausted sister, grim-faced. Greatpaw hung his head guiltily, knowing that much of Ice Eyes's anguish was because of him.

Star sighed and got to his feet. He wanted to distract his siblings. Wagging his tail, he invited them to play.

Greatpaw accepted his invitation immediately, knowing he would win this play-fight as he had all the others. Star had never been a sore loser, and the competitions were always fun for both of them.

Mala jumped in as well, trying to focus on the game. She kept seeing Alric's paw flashing through the air, kept feeling the impact of hitting the ground. Usually, she went off on her own when she was upset, but she couldn't do that this time, not if she wanted to forget.

Soon, the three pups were chasing each other in circles and having a grand time, Ice Eyes quietly watching as she regained her strength.

Greatpaw tackled Mala first, pinning her down as they wrestled ferociously in a patch of feathery grass. After a moment, he backed off so she could get to her feet and jumped at Star. After only a short time, Mala trotted off to sniff around the area, no longer interested in the game. She didn't feel any better than she had before, especially not with Ice Eyes sitting on the sidelines, watching her siblings with an accusatory stare.

Once Greatpaw had pinned Star down a few times, the two males looked around, unsure of what to do. Greatpaw yipped at Ice Eyes, inviting her to join the game.

Greatpaw and Ice Eyes circled each other while Star watched nervously. Both were desperate to defeat the other. Ice Eyes wanted to cement her place as the most dominant pup so that Alric had no choice but to acknowledge it. She wanted to lead the pack someday. If she couldn't be alpha, she would have to leave her home, her parents and siblings, to start a family of her own. Or stay in the Willow River pack and watch Greatpaw live the life she dreamed of ... and *that* she could *never* do.

Greatpaw, meanwhile, felt the need to earn the position his father was thrusting upon him. Ice Eyes may be his sister, but he had a duty to the entire pack to overcome every challenge set before him.

Little Ice Eyes knew she stood no chance in a trial of strength, especially in her present state, so she tried to end the fight before it had even begun. Snarling at Greatpaw, she stood as tall as she could and arched her neck, her tail pointed upwards as a sign of dominance. She needed to show him that she was a wolf to be feared.

Greatpaw understood the message. His sister was ready to fight. But so was he.

They sprang at each other. Greatpaw sailed through the air, aiming to land squarely on top of Ice Eyes, but she rolled out of the way at the last second and he crashed to the ground. Having failed to win with intimidation, she planned to triumph over Greatpaw with speed, agility, and trickery.

Slowly, Greatpaw raised his head. His nose was sore from where it had collided with the grass, and one of his paws was aching.

A wave of satisfaction coursed through Ice Eyes as she watched her brother lying on the ground, winded. She was angry, and her anger gave her the energy to fight on. Even though she knew Alric's behavior wasn't Greatpaw's fault, he benefitted from the injustice. In the heat of battle, Ice Eyes wanted her brother to pay.

She lifted her front paws, ready to slam them on top of Greatpaw's prone form.

But then he did something unexpected. Seeing his sister's attack coming, he lashed out with his paw at her hind leg. With her forelegs up in the air, Ice Eyes was knocked off-balance by the strike and flopped over. Now *she* was the vulnerable one.

Getting to his feet in one fluid motion, Greatpaw

descended on Ice Eyes. Trapping her with a heavy paw, he looked down at her, deciding what to do.

He whipped his head around, hearing a yip from somewhere behind him. It was Alric, watching the fight attentively, an order at the front of his mind. He wanted Greatpaw to teach Ice Eyes a lesson. Alric needed his heir to go unopposed, to end Ice Eyes's pointless ambitions and enforce his will. To do what would please the ancestors.

Greatpaw looked down at Ice Eyes. She was half his size, quivering from exhaustion, and her eyes gleamed with fear and desperation. She was his sister. He backed away.

Greatpaw was now the alpha pup. But his hold on the rank was a tenuous one. He had refused to harm Ice Eyes, and that had given her a narrow opening with which to take back her position.

Ice Eyes lay defeated, but rage still simmered behind her eyes. Greatpaw had beaten her fairly, but something about his victory felt wrong to her. She was being herself, and Alric was punishing her for it. It wasn't her fault that she was small, and female, and more dominant than Greatpaw.

According to the Old Way's teachings, females were inferior and incapable of leadership. Ice Eyes would have to work hard to subvert those beliefs. She wanted to show Alric that *she* was the heir he was looking for. That *she* was the one meant to rule the Willow River pack. She could see from his narrowed eyes that he didn't approve of Greatpaw's mercy. He saw it as weakness. Ice Eyes would show him strength.

She pushed herself to her feet and jumped onto Greatpaw's back, feeling his fur between her claws. His eyes widened in surprise, and he allowed himself to be pummeled to the ground. Ice Eyes slammed her paws into her brother's head, over and over, tail lashing, rejoicing in the ache of her paws as they landed hit after hit. She kept striking until her fury was spent. Then, finally, she stepped away.

Greatpaw raised his head and looked around, dazed. The first things he saw were two slits of icy blue, staring down at him. Quickly, he turned his head away. There was too much malice in those eyes.

He'd walked away to avoid hurting her. But she had betrayed him. And he knew they would never see each other the same way again. How did she expect to rule the pack if she couldn't show compassion or mercy? Ice Eyes was trying to change laws and ignore customs that had protected the pack for generations, and she wasn't doing it for the pack's sake. She was doing it for herself. Greatpaw didn't want to fight his sister, but Ice Eyes was too determined to become leader. He had to win, if only to save the pack from her selfishness and cruelty.

Greatpaw pushed aside the sinking feeling in his stomach and turned towards Alric. When he met his father's gaze, he saw only disappointment.

Lora and Rynna bounded over, sniffing the red-furred pup, concerned. Then, as one unit, they turned to Ice Eyes. Seeing the insolent expression on her face, Lora walked over to her and cuffed her once, hard, on the ear.

She didn't react. Her body was frozen, and her eyes were cold.

Greatpaw got to his feet. He ignored Ice Eyes. Instead, he trotted to his father, met Alric's gaze with his own, and then walked away.

Greatpaw knew that if he was going to achieve his destiny, he'd need his father's help. Maybe it was unfair, but Ice Eyes was too dominant and too determined for her brother to defeat her on his own. However, if Alric wanted to lend his support, he would have to do it Greatpaw's way. And that meant Ice Eyes would not be harmed.

No matter how ruthlessly Ice Eyes fought, Greatpaw would always respond with honor and mercy.

Like a true leader should.

Chapter 15

Alric sat with his claws dug into the grass, a growl simmering at the base of his throat.

He had expected Greatpaw to do everything possible to maintain the highest-ranked position. Yet the foolish pup seemed to think he could win against Ice Eyes without properly putting her in her place.

Alric didn't want Greatpaw to injure his sister. Just teach her a lesson. Ice Eyes was a dominant wolf. Even with Alric's help, a show of force might be necessary to defeat her. But Greatpaw wasn't cooperating.

Alric curled his top lip, exposing a shining row of teeth. He didn't want to spend a second longer than necessary in this place. If Ice Eyes was strong enough to fight Greatpaw, then she was certainly strong enough for travelling. It was time to leave the field and continue the journey to the summer home.

Alric raised his head to summon the pack. Then he stopped, noticing something.

Mala had wandered away from the pack. She was exploring the other side of the field, and it was obvious that she had missed the fight between her siblings. Too curious for her own good, she had gone to investigate a scent she'd never come across before. It had turned out to be a snake burrow, and now she was happily poking around the entrance, covering her wet, black nose in dirt.

What she didn't see was the golden eagle high above her, soaring lazy circles in the sky.

Alric took a step forward. His first instinct was to warn his packmates, but he pushed it down. He had been looking for a way to be rid of Mala without having to fight Lora. Perhaps this eagle was the solution.

Still, he felt a flash of guilt. This was a terrible way for his daughter to die. But her death was necessary. Food had been scarce since the pups were born, enemy packs were encroaching on Willow River territory, and Star had almost drowned in the stream. Such misfortune couldn't be a coincidence, so soon after a cursed pup's birth. The ancestors were angry. They were punishing the pack for letting Mala live this long. If Alric spared her life now, things would only get worse. He took a deep breath and remained silent.

None of his packmates were paying attention to Mala. Lora and Rynna were still fussing over Greatpaw. Ice Eyes had stalked off by herself, and Star had timidly followed her, hoping to cheer her up. Wyanet had joined Alric on the rise and was quietly grooming herself, while Hawk kept his eyes fixed on the alpha male, likely plotting his usurpation.

It was the perfect opportunity. Alric watched as the eagle swooped lower, Mala still oblivious. She continued to sniff the snake's burrow, not bothering to check for danger. She was too far away for Lora to reach her on time, Alric knew. He began panting, finding it hard to breathe. He closed his eyes.

He knew this moment would haunt him for the rest of his life. Lora's quiet grief at the loss of her pup, the anguish of Mala's siblings ... It would be his fault. He thought of his ancestors, of his duty to the pack, but they suddenly didn't seem to matter anymore.

The golden eagle's eyes were fixed on the wolf pup. He was hungry. His rich, brown plumage reflected the light of the afternoon sun as he ducked lower and lower. Then he dove.

Mala heard the rustle of feathers above her and looked up. The eagle was a golden-brown blur speeding towards her, and she stared up at it, wide-eyed. She took a step back, then another, tripping backwards across the grass.

Lora finally spotted the danger and raced towards her daughter. But she wouldn't make it in time to save her.

Star cried out in terror as the eagle extended a pointed,

yellow talon to scoop up Mala. Even at this distance, he could see the tip of the claw, glimmering black against the bright sky.

Mala was a good sister. She intervened on his behalf when play fighting got too rough. She shared pup toys with him, sticks and bits of moss that Ice Eyes hoarded. He didn't want her to die.

Desperation filled him, and he felt a familiar shock travel through his body.

Suddenly, a massive gust of wind swept across the field. It blew Star's fur into his eyes and sent pieces of grass and bits of dirt flying in spirals through the air. It was neither cold nor warm, and it almost lifted Star off his paws, cushioning him upon its soft folds, a pillow of air.

The wind blew the eagle off course. Star heard his angry shriek and whimpered with relief. But with a few flaps of his massive wings, the eagle recovered and prepared himself for another dive.

Right then, Mala knew she had been too reckless, too careless. She should have stayed near the pack. She should have paid more attention to her surroundings.

Were the ancestors behind this? Did they hate her as much as her father did? Did they really believe she had dark powers, that she was evil?

Mala knew she didn't deserve this.

The ancestors were wrong. The other wolves were wrong. Alric was wrong. Mala was ashamed of them. She pitied them for their ignorance. And, more than anything else, she wished she could bring herself to hate them for what they had done to her. How they had made her a pariah in her own birth pack, unwelcome from the moment she stepped out of the den. How her father had jumped at every opportunity to dispose of her, and how her mother had let him abuse her unchallenged. How Hawk and Wyanet had shot her hostile glances, how even her siblings sometimes seemed afraid. All because of the color of her fur, something she had never asked for and could not control.

As the eagle drew closer, and talons stretched out like a yellow net over her vision, the only thing Mala felt was anger.

Something rose up inside her. Something dark.

At first, she thought it was an emotion. But it was too real, too tangible. And it had broken something inside of her, punched through some invisible wall to emerge in all its terrible glory.

She tried to push it back down to the heart of herself, but she couldn't. It fed off her anger, and rose, and rose, and rose. It felt slippery. Vile. Evil. It touched her lungs, her heart, her stomach with its slick fingers. It reached her skin, pressing on it, ripping at it, desperate to escape. And then it exploded outwards.

The eagle began to decay.

It happened quickly. First his feathers fell off in clumps, drifting away on the heavy wind, crumbling to ash. Then his body broke into a thousand tiny flakes, collapsing into a pile of dark powder on the grass. There was something terrible about it, something wrong, just like the shadowy thing Mala had felt only seconds before. The eagle was dead. Nothing but a pile of black dust, like flakes of charcoal long burned out.

Mala was numb.

Alric watched in shock. Mala's eyes were glowing red, veins of black stretching through them, pulsing with menace. They faded back to dark orange as the last of the eagle's remains drifted away on the wind.

It was too late, Alric thought. Mala's powers had awoken. He couldn't kill her. Not now, not ever. If he tried, he might suffer the same fate as the eagle.

He should have acted sooner, should have appeased the ancestors while he had the chance. This was his punishment, and now the pack would fall.

Mala slumped to the ground; all her energy was spent. She sank into darkness.

The entire pack stared at the little black pup, frozen in place.

All except for Ice Eyes. She wasn't looking at Mala. She was staring at Star. Her brother had followed her after she skulked off, probably intending to comfort her. So now, she had a clear view of his shock-filled face.

As the heavy wind wove patterns in Star's white fur, the mark on his forehead glowed.

Chapter 16

The rest of the journey was spent in silence.

The pack passed by a deep valley full of firs, their sap smelling sharp and dull at the same time. They walked through a forest of maples that bowed to them in the wind as they went by. They saw a step waterfall with a current that shone white against dark gray stone and threw up clouds of mist around the shady, moss-lined pool at its base. Weeping willow trees grew from the moss beds, roots hugging the wet rocks and fronds fluttering in the wind as though inviting the pack to stop and rest in the dappled shade.

But Alric couldn't bring himself to slow down, even after the pups started getting tired again. Perhaps if he journeyed long enough, far enough, he could outrun the memory of what Mala had done.

Mala walked behind the other wolves, dark paws dragging on the ground and becoming gradually more matted with dirt and forest debris. No packmate dropped back to check on her, though a few cast nervous glances over their shoulders, worried not for her but for themselves. She was more terrifying to them than ever. And now it all made sense. They had been right about her the whole time, and the realization made her head feel like it was burning. She was tempted to stop walking, to lie down and close her eyes and let them leave her behind. But she was worried that once she stopped focusing on the cyclic movement of her legs, her mind would flutter like a lost bird searching for a perch and would settle back down in the eagle's shadow, where she'd be forced to feel it happen all over again.

So Mala kept pace with the others, and after several more hours of journeying, they arrived at the summer home.

It was a clearing in the center of a dense forest. A boulder sat in the middle, covered in a thick layer of cobwebs and ivy. The dusty ground was littered with pine needles and sharp stones. One corner had a few tightly packed bushes, with space underneath for a wolf to seek shelter.

The pack had been considering finding another summer home for many seasons, but they just hadn't located the right place. This clearing, though it wasn't the most comfortable or the most beautiful, would do. Besides, the pups would spend most of their time exploring the surrounding forest, learning things that would be necessary for their lives as adult wolves. They would study which scents were safe and which to avoid, practice catching small game, and follow the adults to watch them hunt. This clearing served only as a meeting and sleeping place.

The wolves settled in silently, their eyes narrowed and their ears pricking up at the slightest noise. Alric stood atop the rock, sweeping the cobwebs aside with his copper-colored paws. Lora and Rynna cleared out a space underneath the bushes for the pups to stay. Hawk patrolled the edge of the clearing, scenting for danger, while Wyanet swept some of the pine needles out of the way. They worked thoughtlessly and mechanically, movements full of apprehension. Ice Eyes, Greatpaw, and Star tussled near their mother as though nothing had happened. The adults who had protected them their whole lives were debilitated and uncertain. What could the pups do but act like normal, and hope it would all be better when they woke up the next morning?

Mala sat at the edge of the forest, apart from the rest of the pack. She was staring off into the trees, as she had done many times before. But not with the usual glint of curiosity in her rust-orange eyes. This time, there was only sadness and shame. The golden eagle's death kept replaying in her mind. She was responsible for its horrible, unnatural demise. Even though she hadn't meant to use magic, she felt guilty. No creature deserved to die that way, even one who wanted to eat her. She wondered if her father would try to kill her again, and she was frightened. But it wasn't her own life that she was frightened for. It was the death of everyone around her, everyone who tried to prove their devotion to the ancestors by hurting her, that she feared.

Mala didn't want to hurt her father, or her packmates, or anyone else. She wished they would just leave her alone.

She could almost see their faces, outlined among the trees, fading to ash.

And then she felt guilt. Shame. She was just as terrible as they all thought. She had done this.

Suddenly, it was rising in her again. The slimy, sticky evil. Her eyes grew round in soundless shock as she strained to hold it in. But she couldn't. And she was ashamed of that, too. She was trapped, chained within a body that had fur black as night and powers dark as death itself. She couldn't escape it. She couldn't control it.

Overwhelmed, Mala dashed into the forest. She dodged jutting roots and low branches, the wind ripping at her fur, her vision blurring with the effort of holding her magic in. Thorns tore at her sides, but she kept running, trying to escape her family, her powers, herself.

Where her paws landed, the grass blackened and burst into dark, papery shreds, floating away on the wind. And in the shadows between the trees, another wolf crouched unseen, watching the pup race past with eyes of burnt orange, like a pair of embers buried in coals.

Chapter 17

The pine forest was shrouded in shadow. Sharp-smelling boughs reached for Hawk like ghostly paws, their needles tickling his face as he brushed by. The half-circle moon sat swollen in the sky, perched on slow-moving wisps of cloud.

Hawk had wandered off almost immediately after the pack reached the summer home. He had never liked spending time with his irritating packmates, and the strange, gloomy listlessness that had come over them was giving him chills. He had made sure to head away from Mala, who he knew had also gone into the woods. Then he'd begun scenting for prey.

He had hunted for hours as day bled into evening and stars began to poke little holes of light in the black curtain of the sky. Now he was standing between the trees, muzzle raised as he searched for yet another meal.

Hawk needed to become stronger. Challenges over the rank of alpha male in an Old Way pack were serious and often ended in spilled blood. He had planned to challenge Alric very soon, but now that Mala's powers had revealed themselves, he would have to wait. The cursed pup must sense how much Hawk wanted her dead. What if she stepped in to help her father? She possessed an entirely different kind of magic, a rare kind, given to her by the dark ancestors, and Hawk could already tell that it was stronger than his own. Yet he knew from the messages in his dreams that the ancestors were on his side. If they thought he was the rightful leader of the Willow River pack, then surely, he was supposed to challenge Alric. Just not yet.

After all, Hawk didn't just want to defeat the leader. He wanted to *end* him, to finally avenge Lily's death. For that, he needed strength.

Hawk had been surreptitiously eating more than usual from each kill. He was growing larger already. But that wasn't enough. He had to start making kills of his own.

The hunt was the only thing he lived for, now. It was exhilarating. Sometimes he imagined that it was a wolf he was killing, not some innocent elk or deer. Thorn, his cruel sister from the Mud Lake Pack. Alric. Or the cursed pup Mala. And that made it ten times better.

Since the moment Lily had died, Hawk had felt almost dead himself. Lately, his ferocious hunger for a kill was the only thing that could convince him he was breathing.

It was getting even darker, the forest flowing from evening into night. The song of crickets and toads had replaced that of the birds, and now their soft music filled the forest, accompanied by the distant hooting of an owl and the rustle of snakes in the brush. Hawk's dark coat blended with the ridged trunks of the trees, and his yellow eyes penetrated the darkness, focusing on each detail like a bird of prey. He smelled a white-tailed deer and turned to follow the scent, paws making no sound on the pine needles that coated the forest floor.

The deer was grazing peacefully. The shadows masked her light brown ticked fur, and the white markings on her chin and tail glowed in the starlight. Hawk licked his lips, lowered his head, and prepared to attack. He crept slowly forward, taking care not to disturb the grass beneath his large paws.

A second later, he leapt forward. The deer saw him just before he reached her. She dashed away, legs stepping high. Hawk ran after her at a steady lope, conserving his energy. After a moment, she was already far ahead of him. Still, he kept up the chase, staying close enough behind her to see her white tail markings standing out between the pine boughs.

After a few moments, the deer stumbled, too exhausted to keep going. Hawk was on her instantly. His sharp jaws crunched around her hind leg, and he dragged her to the ground.

Hawk ended the deer's life and stood over her carcass for a

moment, deep in thought. Then he began to eat, voraciously devouring his catch.

Suddenly, he heard pawsteps coming from somewhere in front of him. Raising his bloody maw, he sniffed the air.

Two coyotes emerged from the trees. They were thin, their coats disheveled. They hadn't eaten in a long time.

Generally, a pair of coyotes wouldn't risk going near a wolf, especially one defending a kill, and would wait until after the wolves had left the carcass. But this pair couldn't wait. They needed the meat now. Their three pups were waiting back at the den, even hungrier than they were. If they couldn't steal the kill from this fearsome-looking dark wolf, then their young would die.

Hawk glared at them, hoping they would go away so he could eat. They held back for a moment, frightened by the dangerous gleam in Hawk's eyes, but they had no choice. They simultaneously leapt at Hawk.

Hawk didn't even bother with magic. He could do this with his own strength. He swatted the male across the head, sending him flying. The coyote slammed into a tree trunk and slid to the ground, dazed. Then Hawk gripped the female's neck in his teeth and squeezed until she fell dead at his feet.

When the male saw his dead mate, he turned to escape into the forest. But Hawk wasn't about to let him run away. In two short bounds, he caught up with the coyote, pinned him to the ground with his claws, and bit his neck.

With both coyotes dead, Hawk returned to his carcass and ate with satisfaction. He was almost strong enough.

The smell of pups lay heavily on the bodies of the two adult coyotes. Once he had eaten his fill, he turned away, following their scent trail away through the trees.

Chapter 18

Dark clouds covered the mid-morning sky, and Mala sat at the edge of the clearing, facing the trees.

Her pelt was dotted with water droplets that glimmered under the half-obscured sun. Her fur clung to her body, giving her a strange, hollow appearance. The whole clearing was sprinkled with tiny drops of water, turned to gems by the weak rays of sunlight that punched through the clouds. While her siblings played, she haunted the forest's edge, lost in her own lonely world.

Back at the den site, the pups had been forced to stay in the clearing, in sight of their packmates. But now, they could accompany the adults to the elk meadow and watch them hunt or wander away from the summer home to explore the woods, provided they didn't stray too far. Mala could often be found walking between the pine trees, gentle birdsong weaving through the air around her.

Whenever her siblings tried to accompany her, she would warn them off with a sad, angry stare. She wanted them to come. But they couldn't. What if she lost control of her powers again? She'd never be able to forgive herself if one of them was hurt as a result.

Mala often wandered far from the clearing, farther than her siblings were allowed to go. Too far for a packmate to hear any cries for help. Mala knew that she might get hurt out on her own, but she still put herself in danger every day. She wasn't quite sure why she did it. Perhaps she was waiting for one of her family members to intervene, to discipline her for wandering too far as they did her siblings, yet none of her packmates seemed to care. They had already seen her defend herself using her dark powers. But Mala wasn't sure if she'd even try. She couldn't bear to decay anything again and be faced with another bout of crippling, devastating guilt.

During her long walks, Mala often heard a sudden rustle in the bushes or smelled a strange scent in the air. Sometimes it seemed like eyes were staring out at her from the undergrowth. Was she imagining things, or was someone following her? Were there more wolves out there, beyond Alric and Hawk, waiting for an opportunity to finish her off?

Her pack didn't seem to notice her absences. They went on with their activities without her. Every few days, Alric's low, ringing howl would rally the pack for the hunt. Star, Greatpaw, and Ice Eyes would gather with the rest of the pack and join in with high, squeaky voices. Then they would follow the adults to the pack's summer hunting grounds, a small meadow covered in tall grass and wildflowers and filled to the brim with elk.

This place was part of the reason the wolves kept coming back to this particular summer home. These hunting grounds were even more abundant than the ones by the den. The meadow was smaller and shadier, giving them some protection from the brutal summer sun. The grass was tall and soft, with a faint sweet smell the wolves loved.

But Mala refused to go with the pack to watch the hunts, to learn from them. The further she was from her packmates, the safer they all were.

Sometimes Rynna stayed behind with Mala, but other times the pup was left alone at the den site. Since the incident with the golden eagle, Rynna had distanced herself from Mala. Though she still cared about her younger sister, she couldn't help but be nervous around her.

Mala pretended not to mind.

Today was the worst day yet. Even exploring didn't interest her. So, she sat staring at the shadows between the trees, flicking raindrops off her ears.

The drizzle was an annoyance for the wolves. They didn't like getting their pelts wet. But Mala was calmed by the tap, tap, tapping sound of raindrops hitting pine needles. It helped her think clearly.

Greatpaw watched her from the other side of the clearing. His eyes were full of worry, and his tail twitched in agitation as he grappled with his own emotions. As hard as Alric tried to pass down his fear and hatred of wolves like Mala, she was Greatpaw's sister, and he couldn't bring himself to hate her. She looked lonely, and Greatpaw wished he could help. But what if Alric noticed?

Star had tried walking over to Mala several times in the past few days, but he always stopped and turned around before he reached her. Greatpaw hoped Star would find his courage soon, or else the duty of comforting Mala would fall on Greatpaw's shoulders. And he couldn't afford to upset his father right now. Not when he still needed the leader's support to fend off his other sister.

Ice Eyes sat calmly in the center of the clearing, next to Lora and Rynna. She turned her head and noticed Greatpaw, then growled softly, the quiet rumble lost within the patter of the rain.

Greatpaw hated the feelings of anger and animosity that had sprung up between them since their journey to the summer home. He now knew that if he were ever going to become alpha pup, he would have to work for it.

Ice Eyes saw the hard glint in her brother's stare and snorted. Greatpaw was determined, but she wasn't giving up, either. She couldn't let Greatpaw see that their deteriorating relationship bothered her too. She knew he hadn't really done anything wrong, but she still couldn't forgive him for being Alric's favorite. Everything she wanted was given to Greatpaw without him earning it, while Ice Eyes had to work hard just to be noticed next to her brothers. With Greatpaw in her way, she might never be able to lead the pack. She shot a glance at Star, who lay placidly in a patch of weak sunlight, tracing shapes on the ground with his paws. He met Ice Eyes's gaze for a moment, then looked away nervously. He had been avoiding her since they'd arrived at the summer home. She had been the only wolf to notice the gray mark on Star's forehead glowing as wind blew the eagle off course. They had both realized at the same time that Star had magic, magic which first rescued him from the stream and then saved Mala's life. Even though it wasn't dark magic, Star knew Alric wouldn't react well, and he was desperately hoping that Ice Eyes wouldn't reveal his secret.

Ice Eyes dug her claws into the dirt in frustration. If only *she'd* been given powers instead, she could easily have beaten Greatpaw.

After the rock-climbing ceremony, Ice Eyes had decided to change her approach. She would compete directly with Greatpaw, not just at the ceremonies, but all the time. She recognized the threat he posed to her position. She needed to crush it over and over. She needed to show Alric who the strongest pup really was. And she needed to do it soon. Endless dominance squabbles could throw off the long-term balance of the pack.

So, they had been competing. Every day it was something new. Greatpaw had proven himself the strongest. Ice Eyes was the most authoritative. Both were fast and agile. And neither was willing to back down just yet.

A friendly whimper shook them both out of their thoughts. Alric had returned from a short hunting trip with a fat rabbit in his jaws.

Ice Eyes and Greatpaw glanced at each other, then back at their father. And they both decided that they wanted to catch a rabbit just as big as his, if not bigger.

Keeping a pack fed was crucial to its survival. So, if this contest didn't decide who should be alpha, then what would?

Ice Eyes and Greatpaw stalked out of the clearing, heading in opposite directions. The watery sunlight cast a ghostly glow on the forest floor, dappling the ground with light and shadow. The sound of the pattering rain grew louder, and the forest was coated with the scent of damp bark and dewy moss.

The taste of rabbit lay heavily on the air. Ice Eyes and Greatpaw tracked the scent, bodies low and paws drifting lightly over the pine needles, not realizing that the two of them had homed in on the same prey.

They both saw the rabbit at the same time. An eastern

cottontail with brown fur that precisely matched the color of the forest floor. His beady black eyes were fixed on the ground as he foraged.

Then the pups looked up and saw each other. They were standing on either side of the rabbit. He was large, too big for either pup to take down on their own.

Ice Eyes immediately knew what to do. She signaled to Greatpaw with her tail, hoping he would get the message. Then she dashed forward.

The rabbit's head snapped up, and his gaze fixed on the silver pup. He knew Ice Eyes wasn't big enough to take him down. But he spun around and ran, his flight instinct proving stronger than his reason.

Ice Eyes swerved back and forth, herding the rabbit, raindrops from her pelt flying in all directions. A second later, Greatpaw's claws flashed out, his teeth snapped, and the creature was no more. Ice Eyes had chased the rabbit right to her brother. They had worked as a team.

Greatpaw stood, rabbit in his jaws, his mouth filled with the warm taste of its blood. Ice Eyes grinned at him, sizing up their catch. When he tried to grin back, the rabbit slipped out of his mouth, and his sister's smile only widened. Quickly, he scooped the rabbit up again with a wagging tail.

Then a rustle came from the bushes beside them, and Alric appeared.

Ice Eyes raised her head and yapped a proud greeting to her father. She had helped kill the rabbit. Alric would be proud of her.

But Alric walked right past Ice Eyes and approached his son, whining softly with pleasure.

Alric had watched the two pups hunting. He had seen the way they had worked together. But for all Alric cared, Greatpaw had killed the rabbit on his own.

The leader narrowed his eyes, even as he covered Greatpaw with congratulatory licks. After the fight with Ice Eyes during the journey, Alric's son had made it clear that he wouldn't harm his sister. This was the only other way Alric could think of to put her in her place.

He didn't hate Ice Eyes, nor was he plagued by the same confliction that he felt when he looked at Mala. He wanted Ice Eyes to have a happy life. She could help Greatpaw raise his offspring and defend the Willow River pack. If she wanted pups of her own, she could leave, find a mate, and help him start a pack. Then she could concentrate on raising pups, without the burdens of leadership. Burdens that a female such as her couldn't handle. Meanwhile, Greatpaw would carry on Alric's legacy. That was the way it should be.

Alric grinned at his son in satisfaction. He had done both pups a favor. Greatpaw would fulfill his destiny, and Ice Eyes would give up her foolish dreams of leadership.

Greatpaw was hesitant for a second, glancing between his sister and his father, but then he relaxed and dropped the rabbit at Alric's feet. He wanted to make Alric and the ancestors proud. Surely, this was the right thing. The cruel gleam in his sister's eyes had gone out and was replaced with ... nothing. Greatpaw looked to Alric, unsure.

Alric howled in pride and joy. His heir had made the first catch of any of the pups. The rest of the pack, gathered at the nearby clearing, recognized the message and joined in, filling the forest with the celebratory howling of wolves. After all, it was a sign that Alric's heir was meant to lead.

But to Ice Eyes, the leader's true meaning was clear. Only the three of them knew that Ice Eyes had helped catch the rabbit. And it would stay that way, or there would be consequences.

Ice Eyes bowed her head. She was too small and too young to challenge Alric's law. There was no hope for her, not when her father supported Greatpaw so strongly.

She had never felt hopeless before. Not once. But now, the feeling slammed into her like a bull elk's horns. Greatpaw would be the hero pup who caught the rabbit. And someday, the alpha male and leader of the pack. And Ice Eyes would be ...

If Alric had his way, Ice Eyes would waste her life raising pups bound to the same pointless, cruel traditions.

Chapter 19

The sun had not yet risen, and Alric was taking the wolves on a scouting mission.

The ground, deprived of the sun's warmth for a full night, had accumulated a glittering array of dewdrops that were scattered across the grass. They reflected moonlight into tiny pinpricks that stung the wolves' eyes. But the pack barely noticed. They trotted through the forest, dodging bushes and trees, eyes narrowed in concentration.

The Mud Lake pack's border was miles away. The Willow River wolves had needed to leave early so they could reach the other pack's territory before being forced to brave the blistering heat of the afternoon. Alric had no intention of confronting the pack again, not after what happened last time, but he did need to see exactly how often they had been in the packs' shared territory.

The Willow River alpha had smelled Mud Lake scents on the wind, felt a growing hostility on all sides. The other packs had sensed Willow River's weakness. Alric needed to show them that he and his family were strong.

And there was another reason for this expedition, one that only Alric knew about. Many times since the pack had arrived at the summer home, he had gotten the feeling that they were being watched. On several occasions he had caught a foreign scent on the wind and gone to investigate, but he had never found anything. Some mysterious wolf was quite skilled at covering their tracks. Alric had no idea what such a wolf could want from his pack, but he was hoping that a long journey to the Mud Lake border and back would drive them out of hiding.

The pups had never been border-scouting before. Three of them were jumping up and down with excitement. Mala walked several feet to the side, paws dragging. Alric knew it was a terrible risk to take the pups, but it was a necessary one. Rival packs would smell four strong and healthy pups on the move and know that the Willow River pack's future was strong. And the sight of Mala among Alric's family could be enough to scare them away.

Besides, the pups were nearly three months old. They were bold and confident and ready to take on the world. Alric was proud of Greatpaw, Ice Eyes, and Star. And Mala ... Mala was an entirely different matter.

Alric had stopped openly trying to harm her. He had no choice. He couldn't risk going up against powers like hers.

Surely, no member of his pack would blame him after what she had done to the eagle. And in truth, he was relieved that he didn't have to hurt her. Perhaps things could continue this way, but only so long as she never used her dark powers again.

Alric's ears twitched, and he flicked his tail. There was a hum of frustration in the air, and it was putting the whole pack on edge. He whipped his head around, searching for its source. Rynna walked at the back of the group, glaring down at the dewdrop grass, fur standing slightly on end. Alric bared his teeth at her.

Rynna noticed Alric's disapproval but didn't let herself react. She wouldn't give him that satisfaction. The little gray female was rarely angry, yet her father had managed to rile her temper. As a pup sitter, Rynna was supposed to manage her younger siblings. She had to discipline them when they disobeyed her commands, or else they would have no reason to respect her authority in the future. Alric, with his stubborn prejudices, was making everything harder for her.

It had started when Ice Eyes and Greatpaw tried to sneak out of the clearing. After the incident with the rabbit, Ice Eyes had adapted her approach yet again. Now, she was surprisingly civil to her brother and no longer competed with him. Instead, she maintained a rigid dominance over Greatpaw that he didn't dare challenge, knowing that she would show no mercy if he did. She always took the first bite of elk and walked at the front of the little group of siblings, and there was nothing Greatpaw could do. He knew that while his sister might pretend to be over what had happened, provoking her was bad idea. She was beginning to doubt herself, and that made her even more ruthless.

So, when Ice Eyes had smelled an unfamiliar scent at the edge of the clearing, Greatpaw had followed behind, making no attempt to overtake her.

Rynna, from her sunny patch of ground near the center of the summer home, had smelled it as well and recognized it: a lynx and her kits.

If the wolf pups were to go near the mother lynx, she might kill them to defend her own young.

Rynna had leapt to her feet and charged into the forest. A moment later, she walked out again, leading the two wolf pups.

Ice Eyes and Greatpaw had sat in front of Rynna, heads bowed. They'd known they had been too reckless, and that their older sister would have to punish them for it. But Ice Eyes refused to feel guilty. She had raised her head to stare at Rynna with an insolent expression. Rynna narrowed her eyes and brought a paw down over Ice Eyes's ears, making the tiny female squeak.

Rynna lifted her paw again, ready to chastise Greatpaw in the same way. But Alric had seen what was happening from the far side of the clearing and covered the distance between himself and his offspring in three bounds. He'd slammed his claws into the earth between Greatpaw and Rynna, throwing up a cloud of dust. Rynna had stared at him, shocked and furious. She was usually a forgiving wolf, but she took pup sitting incredibly seriously. She'd raised her hackles, arched her neck, and snarled at her father.

Alric had looked at her dubiously, then snapped his teeth next to her muzzle. Instinctively, she turned her head away. Then she slowly sank out of her fierce posture and walked off, dragging her paws.

Alric had stood over his favorite son, feeling satisfied. He had wanted to show his packmates that Greatpaw was his heir, to be respected and revered. In Alric's mind, Rynna had no right to discipline the future leader of the pack without the current leader's approval.

As though nothing had happened, he whined cheerfully at Ice Eyes and led his son away.

Rynna had still been angry when the pack set off on the border patrol, and she was still angry now. Alric was refusing to treat her with the respect she deserved as pup sitter. Her father viewed her as nothing but a disappointment, the omega pup who had happened to survive the flood that had taken the lives of her stronger, worthier brothers. Would he ever see her as anything more than that?

As the patrol continued onward, Alric watched his eldest daughter out of the corner of one green eye. She had challenged his authority earlier. He wanted to teach her a lesson. But he would have to wait for the right time.

When they had almost reached the place where the Mud Lake and Willow River territories overlapped, Rynna stopped the pack with a sharp yip. They slowed to a seamless halt, eyes glowing softly in the darkness like so many different-colored fireflies. Rynna loped to the front of the group, communicating what she had scented on the breeze. A deer, grazing nearby.

The wolves moved forward, muscles flowing like water as they stalked towards their prey. A moment later, they saw it, grazing on the dewy grass, pelt shining in the moonlight.

Rynna stepped aside for Alric to lead the hunt, but he stayed where he was. She started stalking the deer on her own. Lora moved forward to help, but Alric lifted his tail, stopping her in her tracks. The deer grazed, oblivious.

When Rynna realized she wasn't being followed by her pack, she stopped moving and looked back. A soft growl rumbled like an earthquake in Alric's throat. It was clear what he wanted her to do.

Rynna had no choice. She charged the deer, a flash of movement in the predawn grayness, and her quarry bolted. The moon shone behind predator and prey, lighting up the far sides of their bodies and leaving the rest of them in shadow. The only sounds were the rustle of grass and the wolves' low breathing.

Rynna outpaced the deer in a few short bounds. But as she neared the deer's sharp hooves, her confidence failed, and her steps faltered. Noticing her waver, the animal kicked out with both legs, hooves outlined in moonlight. The deer's timing was perfect, and Rynna crumpled to the ground, the dewdrops sticking to her fur, two spots on her chest burning like fire.

Lora and Alric both rushed forward. Lora prodded her daughter with her paws, while Alric whimpered with worry. He hadn't meant for Rynna to get hurt. He had expected her to fail at the hunt and suffer a minor humiliation. But now she was injured, and it was his fault.

Rynna got unsteadily to her feet and shook off her fur, dislodging several dewdrops. Then she turned to look at Alric. He lowered his head. He had made a mistake.

Rynna whimpered her forgiveness and moved forward to lick Alric's muzzle. Alric had learned his lesson. There was no point in holding a grudge. Prey was bountiful this time of year, and the pack would soon catch something else. Rynna's bruises would heal.

But Lora wasn't going to let her mate off the hook so easily. She turned and growled at him, her hackles raised.

The look he gave her in return, one of sadness and remorse, stopped her in her tracks. What was she doing, challenging her mate? They were supposed to be allies. They were supposed to respect each other. And seasons ago, before any of these bad things had happened, they had.

Lora had been wandering along the Willow River border on the day she met Alric. She was hungry, alone, and desperate. Alric and his two sisters were the last of the Willow River pack, and he needed a mate so that the pack could continue to grow and thrive.

They had found each other just when they'd each needed to. For months after, they were inseparable. Alric was delighted with their first litter of pups.

But only Rynna had survived. The one female. And when the next year's litter had consisted of just a single lifeless pup, Alric's dreams of a worthy heir had been close to shattering. Lora had seen how his sense of control was slipping, how he didn't quite feel like a leader anymore. Instead, he felt like a failure. He had let down his father, who had made him leader, and his father's father, and all the other leaders before him.

There was nothing Lora could do to console her mate. And when the third litter, Alric's last hope, had been born …

Alric would do absolutely anything to stay in control of his pack. Including humiliating one daughter, crushing the ambitions of another, and attempting to murder a third.

Lora was fed up.

With her tail held high, she prepared to challenge her mate.

And was interrupted by a strong, clear howl.

The wolves' heads snapped up as they searched for the source of the howl. As one, the pack recognized it. They began to whimper nervously, and the pups shrank closer to Lora's side.

The howl was that of a Mud Lake wolf. The scent of the enemy pack blew heavily on the night wind. They had taken the overlap zone. Now they were clustered at the edge of Mud Lake territory, ready to move in on Alric's pack.

Chapter 20

The pack sat in the middle of the forest for two days.

The only way to keep the territory that was still theirs was by refusing to give up any ground. The overlap zone, now completely occupied by the Mud Lake pack, was just a few feet in front of where Alric lay, head cushioned by ferns.

A rustle resonated through the leaves. Alric's head shot up.

He lowered it again as he saw a male robin pecking the berries off a bush, his red chest standing out against the rich green of forest leaves.

Alric bared his teeth at the bird, and the robin flapped off, unsure of what he had done to deserve the alpha's wrath.

Hawk's sister Thorn paced back and forth along the border. She set each paw down with extreme care, making only the tiniest impact upon the carpet of pine needles and leaves, like a gliding ghost. All the while, she glared at the Willow River wolves. Her pack stood behind her, motionless but ready to fight if need be. Though female leaders were as common as male ones in New Way packs, Thorn was more like a dictator. Her pack obeyed her without question, and that made them even more dangerous.

Neither group had any intention of moving until they got what they wanted, or starvation forced them to go and hunt. For the moment, all they could do was wait.

This was important for the Willow River pack. The Mud Lake wolves seemed determined to conquer their territory bit by bit. The rival pack had seven pups to feed this year, plus twice the number of adults as the Willow River pack. They were going hungry. But this territory had belonged to Alric's ancestors for generations. To give even a small piece of it up would corrupt the honor of his legacy.

So, the packs waited in silence as the noises of the forest crept in around them. The robin returned to peck at the berry bush. A strong breeze made the leaves overhead hiss and the branches sway. One small bough snapped and hung, jagged, by a single wooden strand, then dropped to the earth and landed with a crackling thump in a pile of dead ferns. None of the Willow River wolves reacted. They all sat in silence, eyes fixed on the Mud Lake wolves. Even the pups, usually bundles of energy, were subdued as they clustered around their mother.

It was a smell, not a sound, that got their attention next.

Hawk smelled it first. He was crouched on top of a rock as though poised to strike. His sister's presence, coupled with

Alric's still form lying a few feet away, put him on edge. He let out a low whine as soon as the new scent hit his nose. The scent of male loner heading towards them at a rapid pace. He barked a warning to the others, who all got to their feet. The Mud Lake wolves flinched but didn't move.

Alric, his coppery brown coat gleaming red in the late afternoon sun, ordered the pack to stay on guard. Then they waited, their eyes cutting through the forest leaves.

There was a rustle from behind a tall bush, and a wolf pushed through. He made no effort at silence, dead leaves crunching under his paws as he approached the Willow River pack. He was risking quite a bit, coming before the two groups. Either pack could let the loner join them, but they could just as easily kill him.

The male faced the Willow River wolves, legs stiff, tail hanging by his paws. He could smell Willow River's need for new members to keep their borders secure, but he was still nervous and trying not to show it.

Alric inspected him, striving to ignore Thorn's piercing stare. The Mud Lake wolves watched the proceedings with interest, but they didn't intervene. For them, a new pack member would just be an extra mouth, crammed into a territory already too small to feed them all. And they couldn't try to chase the lone wolf away without giving up their strong position along the Willow River pack's border.

The male's name was Sand. He stood rock-still in a patch of sunlight, the wind tugging at his pale-yellow fur. His eyes were the color of flame, and they were lowered only slightly, sparkling with nervous energy. The Mud Lake wolves slowly got to their feet, craning their necks to see what would happen. Sand didn't raise his head. He didn't dare.

Finally, once he was certain Alric wouldn't kill him, he took a tentative step forward.

Sand allowed the Willow River wolves to become aware of his story as he gradually approached. He was from a pack far away, miles and miles to the west. He had been next in line for the alpha position, but then a forest fire had killed his family. So, he had traveled, looking for a mate to start a pack with, or group that needed more strong members. Now he had found one.

Sand gave Alric a lick underneath his muzzle, a tribute to a strong alpha. Alric had a choice. Would he accept this wolf as a member of the Willow River pack? If he did, it might make the pack stronger … or add another potential traitor into their midst. Alric had enough to manage with a cursed pup, a frustrated mate, Hawk and Wyanet causing trouble, and a strange wolf stalking the pack.

But the true threat, at least for the moment, came from the Mud Lake wolves, who outnumbered Alric's pack two to one.

Alric wagged his tail and howled, welcoming the newcomer.

The pack leapt to their feet, grinning. They bounded up to Alric and covered his muzzle in licks, howling their hearts out. Even the pups jumped over and danced around their father's paws, although Mala remembered herself after a second and slunk several paces away.

The Mud Lake Pack darted into the trees like frightened coyotes. The strong newcomer had scared them off. They would be content with sole ownership of the overlap zone and wouldn't advance further, at least not yet.

Sand joined in the celebration enthusiastically. His nervous, submissive manner evaporated, his fiery eyes blazed bright, and he began running circles around the pack. Rynna joined in. She liked this young, energetic male and wanted to impress him.

As the pack began the short journey back to the clearing, Sand observed the wolves around him. What he saw intrigued him. Alric seemed to be a strong leader, but his hold on the pack was slowly slipping. Hawk and Wyanet wanted power, Lora and Rynna were frustrated with Alric's laws, and the pups, especially the two females, felt confused and betrayed by their father. A change in leadership could be imminent.

Sand grinned to himself at that thought. He would be the perfect contender.

Chapter 21

Mala lay on a patch of grass at the edge of the summer home, watching the eastern bluebird fledglings leave their nest as summer sunlight soaked into her fur. Her packmates howled somewhere behind her, preparing for a hunt. Mala didn't plan to accompany them.

At this time of year, all the pups should be going with the adults to the fields full of elk and watching as they hunted. But Mala felt unwelcome. She didn't know if Alric would let her come. She hadn't even tried.

The high-pitched chortling of the fledglings filled a cloudless sky as blue as the eggs they had hatched from. They were accompanied by a single brown-headed cowbird fledgling, a brood parasite, who the bluebird mother had mistaken for one of her own. The bluebirds twittered and flapped their wings while the brown-headed cowbird sat on a branch and watched, emanating a hollow glugging sound followed by a piercing shriek. Its strange call drowned out the laughing chirp of the bluebirds, and they scattered in a rustle of wings and a flash of blue and red. Perching on branches all around the clearing, they stared nervously at the cowbird with beady black eyes. The cowbird was the strange sibling, the odd one out.

A soft breeze swept through the clearing, carrying a sharp scent to Mala's nose. It was a smell she had become familiar with in recent days. A strange wolf was in Willow River territory, and he had been following her since they'd arrived at the summer home. Mala had been unsure at first, thinking it might only be a figment of her imagination, but after weeks of odd scents, rustling leaves, and the feeling of being watched, Mala couldn't deny it any longer. She stared into the trees, searching for a wolf among the forest's greens and browns, fur beginning to stand on end.

A twig behind Mala snapped, and she whipped her head around, eyes wide with terror. But it was only Lora, trotting towards her with an unreadable expression on her face. Mala relaxed and whined softly in greeting, her tail swishing from side to side over the soft grass. But her friendliness melted away as her mother yipped sharply at her, the sound making the nearby bluebirds twitter in alarm. Mala slowly got to her feet, eyes narrowed.

Lora nosed her daughter in the direction of the gathering hunting party. Alric stood in the center of the clearing, the three other pups at his paws and the pack milling around him. Excitement hung in the air, dangling just out of Mala's reach. She had no interest in this. She lay back down and rested her head between her paws.

A sharp growl brought her to her feet again. The alpha female wasn't about to let her daughter get away with this. If Mala refused to progress at the same rate as her siblings, she might never fully grow up. She was being a coward, and Lora told her so with a series of rapid yips that ordered the black pup to get a move on.

Mala approached the rest of the pack, dragging her paws. Lora walked behind her, encouraging her with little nudges and soft whines.

When Alric saw his cursed daughter approaching, he snarled at her. Mala shrank back, wavering, but Lora gave her a reassuring lick on the ears and glared an accusation at Alric. Then she growled low, so only he could hear. The message was clear. Lora would fight for Mala's sake.

Alric's eyes widened, then narrowed. Lora wasn't usually this aggressive if she disagreed with a decision he made. He would have to watch her more closely from now on.

But it wouldn't come to a fight. Alric was the leader. He had the support of the pack. What could Lora do against that? He yawned, pretending to be bored with the proceedings, but his ears stayed pricked and his eyes stayed fixed on Mala as she went to join the others.

Star ran up to her immediately, greeting his sister with licks of affection. His white fur pressed against her black coat. The two pups were as different as night and day, yet Star accepted her unconditionally. Ice Eyes joined Star. She nosed Mala happily, and for once, her eyes were full of affection instead of anger.

Greatpaw hung back, glanced once at his father, then leapt forward to playfully tackle his littermate.

Pups were wonderful creatures, so carefree. Alric envied them. They knew nothing about leading a pack, about the delicate balance Alric had to maintain between his duties as alpha and his family's happiness. He alone bore the heavy responsibility of ensuring the long-term strength of the pack, and he could not allow the pups to undermine his authority any longer.

He turned towards Mala, ready to drive her away from the hunting party. This was what was best for the pack. It was what the ancestors commanded. And Alric couldn't deny that every sudden movement Mala made, every bright flash of sunlight hitting her orange eyes, made him flinch. He was afraid of what his daughter could do to him and the wolves he cared about. Alric needed to regain control.

He took a step forward, towards Mala.

To find his way blocked by Lora, Rynna, and three pups.

Lora's pale eyes had turned to white fire, and her gray fur

was like smoke. Rynna's stance showed her nervousness, but Lora softly ran her tail down her daughter's flank, steadying her.

The three pups were nearly as angry as their mother. Ice Eyes's own experiences with Alric had taught her how much unfairness and prejudice could hurt, and she wasn't about to let her sister suffer the same. She knew what is was to be hopeless, now. How hopeless might Mala be, after all she had been through? Ice Eyes respected Mala's incredible abilities, even envied them. She wished she could be powerful like that, so no wolf would ever doubt her again. Perhaps someday Mala would help her turn Alric and Greatpaw into the hopeless ones.

Ice Eyes's cold, accusatory stare, full of pain and determination, stopped Alric in his tracks, and he reminded himself not to underestimate his daughter. For a second, he wondered if Ice Eyes was the strongest pup after all. But then he pushed the thought aside. Even if she were a big, strong male like Greatpaw, she could never lead the pack. She was too selfish, too ruthless, and giving her the power she craved would only make things worse.

She was flanked on either side by her brothers. Star, usually such a shy pup, had turned fierce in defense of his sister and friend. He was terrified, ready to bolt at the nearest hint of danger, but at least he was trying to hang onto his last bit of courage, trying to stand up for his sister. He didn't want to just give up, like he had done so many times before. Finally, he was staying strong, if only for a moment.

On the other side of Ice Eyes, Greatpaw snarled up at his father. He was Alric's favorite, but he was still opposing him. He admired Mala. And for once, he wanted to follow his conscience. He wanted to do something that felt right to him, not just to Alric. He knew he wouldn't always be able to resist the power Alric was offering him, to step out of his father's shadow. But for just this once, he could know that he had made the right decision.

Alric stared, dumbfounded, as his own family turned against him.

Mala was surprised, too. Surprised and upset. She had done this. She had torn her family apart.

But as she looked into her father's cold green eyes, she realized that this wasn't her fault. It was his. If she was really the one responsible for everything that had happened, then why were Lora and her siblings standing up for her now?

They didn't think she was a monster. They cared about her.

She would fight for them. She would fight for herself.

Mala pushed past her mother and littermates and stood in front of Alric. Her eyes betrayed her terror and hurt, but still she stood before her father and snarled at him. She was done feeling guilty for what she was.

Alric weighed his options. He could fight his full-grown mate and daughter and four enraged pups, one with unearthly powers. Or he could back down and save this battle for another day.

He had no choice. All the control had been wrested from his paws. Alric lowered his head, and with one final growl, turned away.

Chapter 22

Alric surveyed the elk with a sharp stare, eyes matching the color of the grass. His fur blended in with the jagged stump of a once-majestic spruce tree that sat stubbornly behind him, and his ears twitched in frustration as he scanned the herd for weaknesses. Mala and Lora had gotten the better of him earlier. He had even less control over his packmates than he'd realized. He wouldn't let down his guard again.

And that meant finding the right elk before Hawk did.

Hawk had good eyes and an even better nose. He could pick out a limping deer from across a meadow and smell a sick moose a mile away. He was usually the wolf to select which elk the pack should hunt, and this essential duty helped solidify his position as beta. It also would make it easier for him to challenge Alric.

Alric's eyes narrowed as he watched Hawk inspect the elk herd. The beta stalked back and forth between two trees, his dark fur stark against the bright blue sky overhead. Alric knew Hawk was just biding his time, waiting for the right moment to claim leadership. Alric needed to strike first. He needed to show the pack that he could spot a weak elk just as well as Hawk, stealing the beta's advantage.

The pups sat in a row at the edge of the meadow. They watched as both Alric and Hawk sniffed the air, trying to pick out the weakest prey.

Mala, especially, was intrigued. She had never seen a hunt before. Her initial fears of hurting her packmates or spoiling the hunt for them had begun to dissipate when her mother and siblings had defended her against Alric. She was still nervous, and uncharacteristically cautious, but her terror and self-loathing had started to fade.

Alric acted so confident, searching for the right elk to hunt. Mala didn't understand. He had seemed so defeated back at the clearing. Was his confidence just a mask, hiding everything beneath?

Suddenly, Alric sounded a howl and started the chase. He had scented and then spotted a cow who had recently hurt her left back leg. She walked with a slight lurch, a tiny delay that was extraordinarily tricky to notice. And the combined scents of all the elk in the herd made it difficult to smell her, too. Alric had achieved his goal. For now, he had the upper hand.

Now it was Lora's turn. She was the leader of the hunt. Springing forward, she leapt across the grass, thick-furred tail billowing behind her. She began to gracefully separate the elk into groups, slicing through them as easily as a claw could slice leaves, trying to isolate the injured cow.

The rest of the pack wasn't far behind. They bounded into action, taking their positions on the field of combat. Alric and Hawk ran just behind Lora, ready to provide backup once she caught up to the elk. Wyanet and Rynna looped around, hoping to cut off the cow when the alpha female drove it past them. Sand stood on the sidelines with the pups. Alric didn't yet trust him enough to let him hunt with the pack.

As they sat watching the hunt, Greatpaw absentmindedly chewed Sand's tail, leaving damp, matted fur behind. Ice Eyes scrambled up his back for a better view, claws stinging his skin. They didn't treat him with any respect. After all, he was only the omega.

When Sand had joined, Alric had deemed the pack big enough to have an omega and had given him the role. Now, his sole purpose was to lower the tension that could easily build up in a larger group of wolves. He did this by being as playful and friendly as possible, eating last at kills, and acting as a scapegoat for all of his packmates' anger.

Perhaps Alric had thought making Sand omega would discourage him from challenging the powerful alpha male. Sand didn't intend to remain the omega for long.

He grinned and swatted playfully at the pups as they clung to him like burs. The duties of an omega weren't what bothered him. He was a naturally playful wolf and liked being a peacekeeper within the pack. But Sand was also dominant, with a temperament better suited for leadership. In Old Way groups like Alric's, the omega received no reward or honor for his efforts, even though he was crucial for maintaining unity within larger packs. Instead, he suffered in silence as the lowest-ranking member of the group. Desperate to join the pack, Sand had reluctantly accepted this role, temporarily.

Usually, the pup sitter would watch the pups during the hunt, rather than the omega. But Rynna was a rather good hunter when working in a group she trusted. So, in addition to his many other duties, Sand must forego hunting with the pack.

Even as the pups played with their guardian, they were enthralled by the hunt. Their wide eyes followed the swirling patterns the adult wolves traced in the grass as they broke up the herd into smaller and smaller groups. Finally, Lora had properly isolated her quarry. She charged the elk down, Alric and Hawk at her side.

Rynna and Wyanet burst out of the trees from opposite directions, charging towards the elk. Soon, the pack had formed a circle around their prey and were slowly closing in.

Alric darted forward and seized the elk's injured back leg

in his jaws. Hawk grabbed the other leg. Then Lora moved forward, ready to latch her teeth around the cow's neck and bring her down.

Suddenly, Wyanet sped forward, nearly bowling Lora over, and grabbed the elk's neck instead. The prey fell with a thump, nearly crushing the stunned alpha female, who leapt out of the way just in time.

Wyanet howled softly in triumph, a sound which went almost unnoticed by her shocked packmates. As leader of the hunt, Lora was supposed to deliver the final blow. Was Wyanet challenging her? Lora shook out her fur and took a deep breath. She knew that Wyanet wanted to be alpha female, but the white-furred subordinate hadn't tried to challenge her for a full season. Lora wasn't prepared for this. Yet she was determined to hold onto her rank. She may be fed up with Alric. But she needed to retain her position as his mate, if for no other reason than to be able to protect Mala from harm.

Lora snarled, the sound reverberating across the meadow. Then she moved forward and took the first bite of the kill, the blood and meat warm between her teeth. No one opposed her, though Alric did growl in frustration. As leader of the pack, he was supposed to eat first.

Wyanet just watched Lora feast with cold blue-flecked eyes. Her time would come soon.

Chapter 23

After they had eaten their fill, the wolves collapsed onto the grass and lay there for a few hours, dozing. They wouldn't have to hunt again for several days.

Rynna and Sand lay side by side, noses almost touching. They'd grown quite close in a short amount of time. It had been only two weeks since Sand joined the pack, but he and Rynna had liked each other from the start.

After a couple of hours of napping, Rynna woke. It was mid-afternoon. The air hummed with heat, and the world seemed blurred and stretched to Rynna's waking eyes. Hawk was already up, standing guard over the carcass, his black muzzle coated in blood as red as a robin's chest.

Rynna sneezed as sharp blades of grass prickled her muzzle. Then she glanced over at her packmates. They were sprawled out on their sides, chests slowly rising and falling, grayish mounds in a sea of grass. Wyanet had wandered off somewhere, but other than that, the pack slept silently.

Rynna glanced to the side and noticed Sand dozing a few

feet away. He was already thinner than he had been before joining the pack. Usually, living as part of a group was easier than trying to survive as a loner, but not for an omega. Rynna felt a flood of sympathy for her new friend. She wished things could be different.

She got up and poked him with her paw. The cream and gray male raised his head, yawning, then blinked his bright eyes open and grinned at Rynna mischievously.

Rynna play-bowed at the omega. Sand play-bowed back. The game was on.

They ran back and forth between the pines, nipping at each other's tails. Their excited yips woke the pups, who immediately joined the game. Soon a long string of wolves and pups extended out over the conifer woods, attempting to catch the wolf in front of them. The trees raced by, blurs at the corners of their vision, and pine needles clawed at their backs and sides. Finally, Sand skidded to a stop, exhausted. He was immediately bowled over as Rynna crashed into him, and soon the pair were wrestling, the pups running circles around them and yipping in excitement.

After a moment, the two of them flopped over and lay there, chests heaving.

Sand looked at Rynna and grinned, tail thumping on the peaty pine-forest ground. She copied him, then rolled onto her back to let her belly soak up the sun.

Before Rynna, Sand had never met a wolf who could match his excitement for games. Sand had always loved to play, but his old packmates hadn't approved of his pup-like antics. They had wanted him to pay attention, to be serious and cautious, so he could lead the pack someday.

Alric was attentive. He was serious and cautious. But even a newcomer like Sand could tell that the pack was falling apart. Perhaps a different style of leadership was needed to keep this family strong. Could Sand be the right wolf to pull the pack back together? He had always wanted to lead.

Sand licked Rynna's cheek and got to his feet, tail wagging. He could take advantage of the Willow River pack's instability. If he seized leadership from Alric, he and Rynna could rule together.

But as Rynna stood up and shook herself off, he had second thoughts. What would his new friend think if he overthrew her father? Wouldn't that destroy her family further still?

Sand raced back towards the meadow with Rynna and the pups, still without answers.

Alric heard the commotion and yawned wide, baring needle-sharp teeth. He had no interest in play. Looking around, he noticed Wyanet's absence and howled, asking her where she was. The low, rich sound rolled through the forest like thunder, and the trees, bending in the strong wind, seemed to be leaning away from it in fear. Alric licked his lips, pleased.

Wyanet heard his howl. She had traveled far in the hour since she had wandered away, farther than she'd intended. Now she was sitting under the willow fronds at the edge of the step waterfall they had passed on their journey to the summer home. It was a hot summer day, and the mist and flickering shade helped Wyanet escape the warm winds blowing up from the south. The rushing water was like a curtain of white fur, and she could see her reflection as she lay in a bed of moss. The edges of her form wavered as the water rippled, reducing her eyes to blue-gray smudges in the pool's surface.

Reluctantly, Wyanet stood and returned Alric's howl. Her voice was high, strong, and gorgeously melodic, reaching up to dance with the birds in the sky. Several miles away, Alric heard it, grinned, and began loping steadily in Wyanet's direction.

Alric moved quickly, reaching her less than an hour later. She hadn't moved from her place under the willows, and was gazing, transfixed, at the glassy water.

Alric sat down beside her so their fur touched, the cold, smooth scent of falling water filling his nose. He closed his eyes and listened to the pounding of the waterfall on the rocks, feeling the spray penetrate his fur and cool his skin.

The hunt had tired him out, and his nap in the exposed meadow with the sun cooking him inside his fur had left him feeling itchy and lethargic. This place reminded him that he was alive.

Wyanet turned her head to look at him, regarding him with that unknowable stare of hers. Both wolves could feel the sacredness of the waterfall and the pool, and they dared not disturb it. They sensed the bright eyes of the ancestors looking down on them, sending down comfort and strength from the sky. So, they sat side by side in happy companionship beneath the willow trees.

Chapter 24

A week passed. The warm winds faded away to nothingness, just an occasional breeze floating through the stagnant summer air.

The wolves gave up all pretense of doing anything during the daytime. They had become completely nocturnal creatures to avoid the oppressive heat. The night was quiet and still, and the cold couldn't penetrate the wolves' thick fur.

Luckily, the borders had remained well-protected. The surrounding packs had been deterred when Sand joined. The addition of a strong male tipped the balance of power just enough to make Willow River territory not worth fighting over. And Alric's frequent patrolling of the border hadn't hurt.

But this fragile peace couldn't last forever. Alric smelled North River scents on the wind. They were on the move.

The North River Pack was Willow River's western neighbor. The stream that sped past the Willow River den site came from a much larger river that flowed southeast through North River territory, branching off into several smaller creeks and streams as it went.

The Willow River and North River packs had an overlapping section of territory rich with game, grassy and open and perfect for a hunting ground. Neither group had dared move upon this land. Until now.

Alric was lost in his thoughts as he gathered the pack around him, preparing to depart for the North River border. The pups shivered with excitement, delighted that their father was yet again bringing them along. They needed to learn what it took to defend a large territory from greedy neighbors. Besides, it wasn't safe to leave them behind. A mysterious wolf was still hanging around the clearing. The more Alric tried to learn his identity, the more skilled he seemed to become at remaining undetected.

Perhaps the wolf was a North River spy. Sending a scout so deep into Willow River lands was a blatant violation of wolf code, but Alric wouldn't put it past the rival pack.

Alric hated this pack above all the others. As he licked himself clean before the patrol, it was as though he were preparing for war. While he and the North River alphas faced off, he mentally readied himself for a fight.

For hours, the two packs stood opposite each other in the center of the overlap zone, growling and baring their teeth. The North River alphas, Pine and Daylight, were unflinching as they stared at Alric.

The pups stood behind Rynna, their fur pressed together as they watched with wide eyes. They had seen similar encounters with rival packs before, none of which had ended in real violence, but this still made them nervous.

It was the dead of night, and starlight filtered down through the branches of the deciduous trees. The full moon bounced light off the wolves' pelts, turning them to shining silver. Rynna, who was crouched in front of the pups, had fur of rippling gray-blue light.

It felt as though a thin sheet of icy silence coated the ground. A single wrong step and it would crack.

Ever so quietly, they observed the enemy pack. They could feel their father's anger and hatred. It made the very air prickle painfully against their skin.

Mala was curious. Alric was keeping the reason for his feelings hidden behind the outer layer of his mind. She narrowed her eyes and observed the enemy pack.

She could gain most of what she needed through scent alone. There were seven adults in the North River Pack, the same number as in Willow River, but one had remained at the pack's summer home with Pine and Daylight's five pups. The wolves here tonight were healthy. They hadn't eaten in a while, but their pack wasn't suffering from the unrest and power struggles that plagued the Willow River wolves.

Mala noticed the scents that wove around the alpha male

and female. Pine, the dark brown alpha male, was larger and stronger looking than his mate. But the alpha female, Daylight, was calm and focused. Her eyes were so pale, they were almost white, and they shone in the night like fireflies. She flicked her tail, an almost imperceptible motion, and the pack moved forward with a collective growl.

Mala's eyes widened. Daylight was the leader of this pack. She nudged Ice Eyes, imparting this information, and her sister sat bolt upright, head tilted to the side in confusion. Could a female truly lead a pack without relying on her packmates' fear of her, as Thorn did? Why hadn't Alric or Lora taught them about this?

Star stepped forward and let his pelt brush against Mala's, holding another strange observation at the tip of his consciousness. The North River omega, whose silver coat shone under the moonlight, smelled well-fed and content. Meanwhile, Sand sat with a bowed head behind the pups, his fur disheveled and his ribs showing through his skin.

Sand's friendly, playful personality had evaporated in recent weeks. Now, after a month of being used as a scapegoat and eating last at kills, he was always angry. But while the North River omega had the same essential duties, she seemed to enjoy a much higher status and was treated like just another member of the pack.

Star felt something close to envy as he watched the rival

pack. He had always been submissive, and he'd wondered if he would be the omega someday. Why couldn't he be treated with the same fairness and respect as the North River omega?

As the cold night drew on, the pups pondered their observations with narrowed eyes and flicking tail-tips. They didn't quite know what to think.

Suddenly, a flash of darkness caught Mala's attention. One of the North River wolves had stepped out of a shadow and was now standing under the full light of the moon.

He was pure black.

He didn't smell different from the others. Mala had realized long ago, from reading the outer thoughts of her siblings, that her own pelt carried a different odor from that of her packmates. It was the scent of fear, shame, and rejection. But this wolf was the beta of his group. He seemed healthy and happy. His packmates *trusted* him.

A shiver ran through Mala's body at the thought of the life she could have led, the acceptance she could have found, were she born into a different pack. Of the life she might still be able to lead, if Alric wasn't alpha.

The North River pack must have abandoned the Old Way. There was no other explanation for their complete rejection of all the ancient laws of the wolf. No wonder Alric hated this pack so much. In his mind, they were committing a gross act of sacrilege by leaving behind the code of the ancestors.

The North River wolves had replaced the Old Way's rigid customs and beliefs with something better. Mala could read it on the edges of their minds, now that she knew what to look for: The New Way.

Mala had already known that Hawk's old pack, as well as Sand's, had followed something similar to this. But the Mud Lake pack's leader had only used it as an excuse to give herself more power, while Sand's old family members were dead, killed by a forest fire. Mala hadn't been able to learn anything else about the New Way, no matter how often she probed the outer layers of her packmates' minds. Alric growled and bristled whenever anyone openly thought about it, and no wolf wanted to provoke him.

But now, the four pups were seeing the New Way for themselves, and one question overtook their minds. Why did the Willow River pack refuse to change? Why did they hold onto their ancient superstitions and biases when these beliefs hurt the wolves within and around the pack? It was a question Mala could not answer.

Alric and Daylight stood snarling at each other for several more minutes, the grass under their paws ripped to shreds by their exposed claws. Alric's fur rippled and gleamed, and his bared teeth shone in the moonlight. He crouched under the open sky, the ancestors' light pouring down and making every hair on his pelt glow. Daylight stood beneath the trees, swathed in shadow, her face as calm as still water and her eyes hard.

Both packs were strong. There was no denying it. And neither could best the other without their own wolves being injured or killed.

So, it came down to which pack could stand there the longest.

The glow of the North River wolves' eyes winked out as they turned away one by one and slipped off into the trees. The Willow River pack had just caught an elk and gorged themselves, but it had been several days since the North River wolves had eaten. They couldn't afford to stay here all night while there was hunting to be done elsewhere. Their pups were waiting back at the clearing for them to return with food, and they wouldn't let them down.

A good alpha knew when to admit defeat. With a final glare cast in Alric's direction, Daylight slunk into the forest.

Alric turned to leave. For now, his territory was safe.

Then Lora began to whine and sniff the air. Alric tilted his head at her, worried. And then he realized what was wrong.

The pups were gone.

Chapter 25

The pups walked through the forest, trailing Coal, the pure black beta from the North River Pack.

They had followed him out of curiosity. At least Mala had. After catching his scent on the air again, she had felt a spark of recognition. She'd caught tiny whiffs of the same smell many times in the past, while walking through the forest by the summer home. Could this be the wolf who'd been following her all this time? She had slipped after him, away from her pack, determined to know the truth.

Star had seen her sneaking off and come with her as backup. And when Greatpaw and Ice Eyes saw them leaving, they had eagerly bounded to the front.

It didn't take Coal long to realize that the four pups were following him. They were noisy little things, stepping on every leaf in their path, and he could smell them clearly. He was well-acquainted with their distinct odors after shadowing their pack for so long. They hadn't yet learned to mask their scents by rolling in feces or a decomposing carcass, as he had often done while tailing them.

Coal and his North River packmates had sensed the unrest in the Willow River pack shortly after Mala was born. Such monumental news as the birth of a pure black pup could not remain contained in the minds of the Willow River wolves, try as they might to conceal it. And when rumors of Mala's burgeoning powers had reached him, Coal had set forth to investigate. She was the only wolf like him he had ever encountered, and he knew how Old Way packs usually dealt with bearers of their kind of magic.

After seeing how she was suffering, he had devised a way to help her. This was his perfect opportunity. He stopped in the middle of a small clearing, wagging his tail and grinning at the pups to let them know they were safe. They hung back, peeking out from behind the tree trunks with wide eyes.

Mala was the first to step forward, boldly striding to the center of the clearing. Her siblings followed her more cautiously.

Trees surrounded the clearing, oak and beech, chestnut and elm. At its center was a pair of conifer saplings, the same height as the wolf pups. The moon shone bright on the saplings, highlighting their every slender needle in pale light.

Coal sat across from the pups, on the other side of the saplings, in the shadow of the trees behind him. His eyes were closed tight, and without the dark orange irises standing out against his fur, he was like a solid wall of black. He was concentrating hard on something, though what it was, the pups could not tell.

Suddenly, Coal opened his eyes. They glowed blood-red, black veins pulsing through them from the strength of Coal's magic. Shadows surged outwards from around his body. Not the natural shadows created by the dark, moonlit night, but strange and twisted ones, emanating from Coal himself. Thin rays of darkness, rippling and folding in on themselves, rendering the whole clearing an absolute black. The pups could not see each other. They could not see their own paws beneath them, or the pine saplings that had seconds before been bathed in moonlight. All they could see were two slits of red in the blackness, like twin drops of blood suspended in the void.

This was not the decaying magic that Mala had used on the golden eagle. It wasn't destructive. Nevertheless, it was terrifying. Ice Eyes's gaze hardened, Greatpaw took a step back, and Star started whimpering. But Mala stood frozen. She didn't know what to think. Although the shadows felt slightly less malignant than the decay, they were still dark, and evil, and wrong.

With a whooshing sound, they slipped away as quickly as they had come. The clearing was exactly as it had been before, and Coal grinned at the four wolf pups as though nothing had happened, as though he had just done something *good*. And then he was whimpering at Mala enthusiastically, inviting her to try.

Before her family had stood up for her, before they had forced Alric to let her watch the hunt, Mala would have fled this clearing without looking back. But now, she felt more confident in herself. Besides, how much harm could shadows really do? So, she sat and closed her eyes and concentrated, and the shadows answered her call.

It was the same vile black magic, but this time *she* controlled it. She drew it up from within her and sent it outward, knowing exactly what she wanted to happen. And when she opened her eyes, the shadows were there.

She could feel the magic draining her energy. She could only maintain this for so long. With a deep breath in and out, she let the magic slip away.

With a wave of his tail, Coal communicated to Mala what he knew. As long as she remembered that it was shadows she'd wanted, and not the decay, her magic could be controlled. She must keep her emotions in check. If anger or fear took hold, the decay would return, just as powerful and irrepressible as before.

Her siblings stared at her with a mixture of respect and fear in their eyes. Mala could access her powers without unleashing destruction. At least for now.

Then Coal closed his eyes again, and one of the pine saplings began to disintegrate.

All four pups backed away as fast as their paws would carry them. The sapling was just a pile of ash now, blowing away on the wind. *This* magic was dangerous. It could kill. It scared all four of the pups, Mala most of all.

Coal watched the pure black pup. His grin was gone. He had noticed her reaction to the decay, and his gaze was tinged with sadness.

Mala growled low in her throat. She wanted no part in this type of destructive magic. It felt darker than the shadows, as though it was a manifestation of death itself. Maybe Coal had learned to control it, but she had not. And she wouldn't risk her siblings' lives for power's sake.

Coal grinned, reassuring her, inviting her to use her powers. If the decay got out of control, he could stop it. Her siblings would be safe. With a shrill yip, he urged her to step closer to the other pine sapling. The closer she was to it, the more power she could direct towards it.

Star was the first to whimper his encouragement, and the other pups joined in. If Coal wanted to harm them, he would have done so already. They trusted Mala. Why couldn't she trust herself?

Mala sighed, relenting. If she was going to have magic, she might as well know how to use it. She stepped forward, closed her eyes, and concentrated, reaching for the black well within herself where her powers lived.

And nothing happened.

For the next few minutes, she tried and tried to decay the sapling in front of her. But no matter how hard she focused, there was no result. What had happened to the feeling of raw power, rising within her until it boiled over? It was gone. The black magic had retreated deep inside her, too deep for her to find. Her own fear had driven it away.

Mala whimpered, relieved. She stood and returned to her siblings.

Suddenly, Ice Eyes had an idea. She remembered standing in the field, watching the golden eagle swoop closer and closer to her sister, and then seeing the glowing mark on Star's forehead as the wind swept the bird off course. Even further back, she had watched in terror as Star was swept downstream towards sharp rocks, only to wag her tail in relief as he had inexplicably flown to safety. Her brother had powerful magic, and if there was any wolf who could teach him how to harness it, it was Coal.

Grinning, she nudged Star towards the pure black male.

Star hung back for a moment, hesitant to reveal his abilities to Mala and Greatpaw. What if they let his secret slip? Alric saw all magic as a threat to the order of the pack. Star's powers weren't like Mala's, but that didn't mean he wouldn't be treated differently for having them. Star wavered, unsure, until both Greatpaw and Mala encouraged him with soft whines and brushes of their tails. They had no intention of betraying their brother.

Star closed his eyes and concentrated just as Coal and Mala had done a moment before.

The mark on his forehead glowed bright, and wind whipped through the clearing, swirling the wolves' fur and blowing leaves in circles through the air.

The pups stood in silence for several moments, marveling at Star's hidden ability. His magic wasn't dark at all. The wind he had conjured was warm and gentle against their fur.

Star stared wide-eyed up at Coal, shocked at what he had just done, how he was so easily able to control the power within him. The power to keep his siblings safe. The power to command his own fate? Perhaps the future would hold something more for him than being an unvalued and underfed omega.

Mala hung her head. For a moment, jealousy seethed within her. Like her, Star had powers beyond those of most wolves, but he would never be hated or feared or judged for them. His abilities were a talent. The unfairness of it ... she'd decay this whole forest if it meant leaving her own cursed powers behind.

But Star had always been the kindest of her siblings, the

one who stood up for her and cared about her no matter what she did. And this power had saved her life. She forced her fur to lie flat, pushing her jealousy aside and letting herself be happy for Star. It was her own magic she had a problem with.

Suddenly, Coal flinched, his eyes flashing. In his eagerness to teach the pups what he knew, he hadn't noticed the telltale odor of their pack, swirling closer and closer on the wind. Now it was too late. Their scents were sharp on his nose, too close to be overlooked, coming from all around him.

With a farewell wave of his tail, he turned and bolted towards the trees. But his way was blocked by a large, dark-furred form, golden eyes nestled above snapping teeth. Hawk.

Coal stumbled back, looking for another way out. But more wolves were leaping from behind bushes and trees, blocking his escape routes, closing in around him and the pups.

Alric was the last to emerge from shadows. His eyes were fixed on Coal. The pure black beta of another pack had dared to abduct the alpha's pups. Now Alric would make him pay.

Chapter 26

For a moment, no wolf moved.

Alric's gaze darted between Coal and the pups, the moonlight and darkness muting his eyes to a glassy gray-green. He was afraid. Afraid that his family would get hurt, that the pure black Coal would use his dark powers against him. Afraid that all the control would be wrenched from his paws yet again.

Alric had only ever wanted to be a good leader, to stay true to the Old Way and keep his pack safe. Where had it all gone so wrong? Why were the ancestors torturing him like this? First Mala's birth, then the revelation of her powers, and now this terrifying, black-furred stranger. The world seemed determined to ruin Alric, to strip away all his power and strength. He didn't feel like a leader anymore. He felt like a rabbit, a piece of prey, squirming beneath the claws of the fear that had ruled his life since Mala emerged from the den.

The whole world wanted Alric to fail. Today, he would prove them wrong. If Coal decayed him, at least he would die honorably, not clawing after his fading power like a mouse scrambling for seeds.

He stepped forward, signaling for his packmates to do the same. Only Hawk obeyed. The others hung back, eyes wide with fear. Lora crept to the far edge of the clearing, then yipped at the pups, who moved hesitantly to her side. With a whine, she urged Alric to back down. The pups were safe now, and Coal crouched low to the ground, his posture almost submissive. He seemed in no hurry to attack the Willow River wolves. But if they provoked him, his dark magic might kill them all.

Alric ignored his mate's warning. He leapt forward, reaching the center of the clearing in two bounds and bringing himself face to face with the smaller male. Coal didn't even flinch. His eyes pulsed a faint red, a malevolent beat that echoed the drumming of Alric's own heart. But resignation buzzed near the outskirts of Coal's thoughts, and he kept his fur flat. He was giving up. He wouldn't even fight back.

Alric grinned in satisfaction. Perhaps Coal had realized the evil of his own existence and was willing to repent. Or maybe he was just tired of fighting. Either way, this was Alric's chance.

Black flashed in the corner of his vision as Mala threw herself between him and Coal. She had to look up at her father to meet his eyes, but he took a subconscious step back

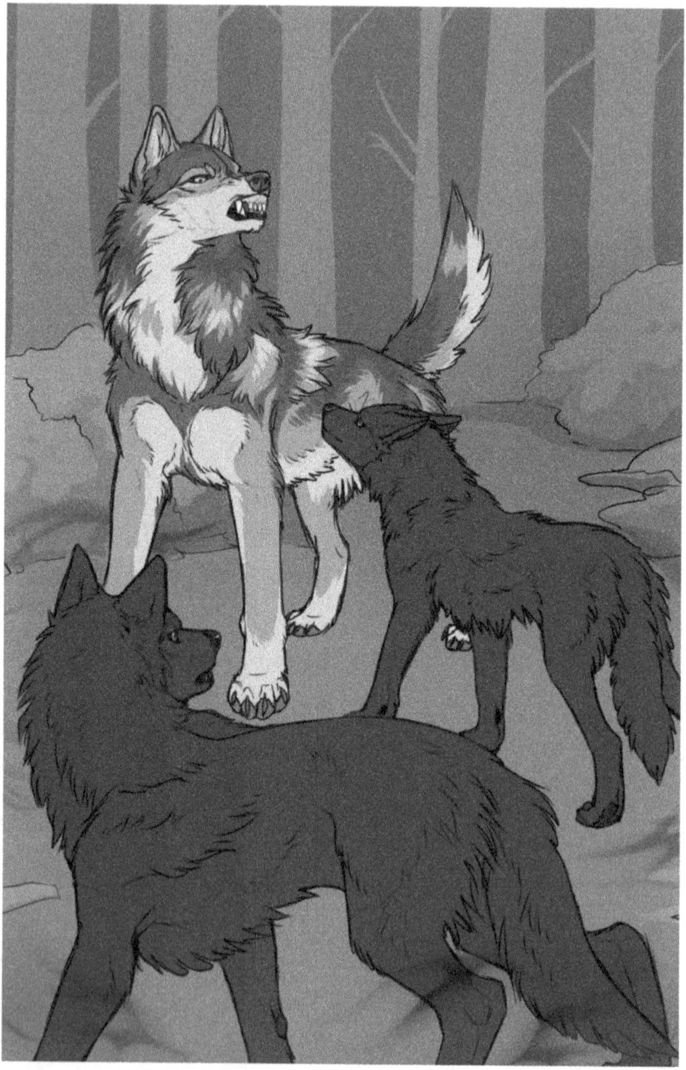

when he saw the fury in her stare. She was still a pup, but she didn't seem like one, not with her fur billowing like a dark halo around her face. Her gaze didn't waver, not even when Lora whined frantically, ordering her to return to her siblings. Not even when Alric growled deep in his throat, eyes angry slits in his head.

Mala wasn't his daughter in this moment. She was the enemy. She and Coal might as well have been different-sized copies of the same wolf, with their matching onyx-black fur and sleek frames. Of course she was siding with him. They had the same evil purpose in this world, serving the dark ancestors and ruining everything Alric had built.

Coal nudged Mala to the side, out of danger, but she just stepped back in front of him, even more determined than before. Alric could tell from Coal's scent that he was the wolf who had been spying on the Willow River pack. How long had Mala known his identity? How long had they been conspiring to abduct the other pups, to take away what Alric held most dear?

The leader growled again. It was Mala's last warning.

She stepped forward, closer to Alric, and snarled in his face.

He pounced, slamming her to the ground, tearing at her fur. All he could hear was the pounding of his own heart and the blind fury roaring in his head.

For a moment, Mala fought back, squirming in her father's grasp. But then all the fight flowed out of her like fading rain after a storm, and her body went limp. Alric was more than twice her size. The only way she could defeat him was with magic. Dangerous, dark, evil magic. She would rather be ripped apart by claws and teeth than feel the guilt of using such a thing against her own father. And she wasn't even sure if it was possible, not after the last time she had tried. She would let him punish her.

Alric and Mala could hear Hawk's vicious growling and the frantic whimpers of Lora and the pups. But it all seemed to be coming from very far away. Father and daughter were lost, he in his rage, she in her despair.

Then they heard a sound that snapped them back to life, a *whoosh* that echoed through the clearing like a tempest blowing in.

They were surrounded by darkness. Flickering, billowing darkness, with a life of its own. But it wasn't Mala who had summoned it. Outside the dense ink-black sphere that encased her and Alric, Coal's eyes glowed red. He wouldn't use his powers to defend himself, but he could not sit by and watch an innocent pup get hurt.

Alric scrambled away from Mala and charged towards the pair of crimson lights beyond the black haze. Coal stumbled back, unprepared for the quick retaliation, and the circle of darkness fractured. With a second surge of power, he brought up a wall of black between himself and Alric, but the furious leader leapt through it without hesitation. The two males faced each other, this time with no one to stand between them.

The clearing was silent. No magic now, just the natural light of the moon filtering through the forest leaves. Mala stayed where she was, crouched on the grass, feeling more powerless than ever. Alric took one step towards Coal, then another. The other three pups began to whine, pleading with their father to leave him alone.

Alric ignored their cries. Coal was smaller and weaker than the Willow River leader. And he wouldn't decay him. This was Alric's chance. Why shouldn't he take it?

Coal deserved to die. The ancestors decreed it. Alric would make it slow and painful, so Coal understood how the leader had felt when his pups had gone missing, when he hadn't known if they were safe.

Alric clamped his teeth around the neck of his enemy and bit down.

Mala turned her head away. She didn't want to see.

When she looked back again, Coal was lying still, the light in his eyes already beginning to fade, like a fire dwindling to ashes. Alive, but not for long.

Was this Mala's fate? Would she someday have to choose

her own death, in order to avoid decaying another wolf? Or would she kill to save herself?

Frozen in place on the gray moonlit grass, she watched as Alric gathered the pack on the edge of the clearing. They needed to be far from the border before the North River pack found Coal's body and decided to take revenge. But Mala couldn't bear to accompany them. She would stay with Coal in his last moments. It was the least she could do, after everything he had taught her.

The only wolf she had met that was like her, probably the only one she'd ever meet ... and she was already losing him.

Lora and the other pups glanced back at Mala as they followed Alric into the trees. But they didn't call out to her, didn't try to make her come along. They knew that from now on, she'd have to make her own way. Even if she chose to return to the pack, she would never fully be part of it.

Mala watched as the Willow River wolves slipped one by one into the forest and were swallowed up by the night.

When she turned back around, Coal was standing up. His eyes were bright, and his fur shone a solid, untainted black. There wasn't a single drop of blood on the grass.

He was healed.

In a flash of black, he disappeared between the trees.

Mala was left alone in the clearing, stranded in the cold, still light of the moon. She couldn't even begin to understand what had just happened. But something was lifting her up, a ghostly thread to the stars, telling her she wasn't alone. Because Coal had survived, and perhaps the ancestors were on her side after all. She had to find him. She had to find answers. And once she had done that, she would return to her family and fix everything that had been broken. Alric might try to drive her off, but Mala had a mother and siblings who accepted her, and she wouldn't let him take that away from her.

With one last look at where her family had gone, Mala took her first steps into the uncertain night.

Acknowledgements

I honestly have no idea how this has happened, but I do know that it wouldn't have been possible without a great number of incredibly caring and talented people:

Mom, this book (and I) would not be here without you. Thank you for reading it an unholy number of times, for your invaluable feedback, and for every other thing you do that I don't appreciate nearly enough. And thank you, Dad, for being the greatest advocate I could ask for, and for never giving up on me.

Tremendous thanks to my agent, Stephanie Rostan, for taking a chance on me; to my editor and publisher, Georgia McBride, for your tireless work and mentorship, and to everyone else at GMMG. Thank you for your patience in guiding my teenage girl self through this process. As cliché as it sounds, you have made a dream come true.

To Inigo, who introduced me to all the best books. I will be eternally grateful for your friendship, your creativity, your ideas, and your unwavering support. To Maya, for keeping me sane and for telling me I'm being an idiot when I'm being an idiot. And to my brother, Jack, for motivating me and always having my back.

I would also like to thank the writers Erin Hunter and Katherine Lasky, who filled my childhood with animals, forests, and magic. And the late, great Jean Craighead George, whose books were the inspiration for this one. Thanks also to Joey Soloway, Thomas Lennon, Brian Koppelman, and Soman Chainani.

Thank you to all the teachers who have helped me along the way: Mr. Park, Ms. Roman, Mr. Wilson, Dr. Rado, and so many others. Your support and mentorship have made me the writer I am today.

I also want to acknowledge the International Wolf Center for providing me with the information and resources necessary to write this book, and Wolf Connection for letting me visit. Wolves are constantly at risk of being killed by hunters and driven from their territory by human expansion. Go to <u>nrdc.org/save-wolves</u> to learn more about how to help them.

Nicole Austen

Nicole Austen is a writer and college student from Los Angeles. Since elementary school, she has dreamed of becoming an author, and spent her summer vacations working on novels. A lifelong love of animals and fantasy inspired her to begin writing the Shadow of the Pack duology when she was thirteen-years-old, a draft of which won a National Scholastic silver medal for novel writing in 2019. Besides writing, Nicole loves hiking, playing piano, and spending time with her family and dog.

CPSIA information can be obtained
at www.ICGtesting.com
Printed in the USA
BVHW052244260622
640711BV00003B/9

9 781951 710699